D0382089

Jun 21

THE PRODIGAL
DAUGHTER

Also by Mette Ivie Harrison

The Bishop's Wife

His Right Hand

For Time and All Eternities

Not of This Fold

THE
PRODIGAL
DAUGHTER

Mette Ivie
Harrison

Copyright © 2021 by Mette Ivie Harrison

Published by Soho Press, Inc.
227 W 17th Street
New York, NY 10011

Library of Congress Cataloging-in-Publication Data

Harrison, Mette Ivie, author.
The prodigal daughter / Mette Ivie Harrison.

ISBN 978-1-64129-245-0
eISBN 978-1-64129-246-7

LCC PS3608.A783578 P76 2021 | DDC 813'.6—dc23
LC record available at https://lccn.loc.gov/2020052768

Interior design by Janine Agro, Soho Press, Inc.

Printed in the United States of America

10 9 8 7 6 5 4 3 2 1

For Austin,
who played games with us every night of the pandemic

And to Kristen Mitchell,
who created Youth Futures for just such teens
as Sabrina and Austin

THE PRODIGAL
DAUGHTER

PROLOGUE

Kurt and I were in marriage therapy again. We'd started coming every Monday at noon during his lunch break from work. He'd chosen the therapist, Dr. Candice Zee, a woman working for the Family Services arm of the Mormon Church—a term I technically wasn't even supposed to use anymore, since President Nelson had deemed all nicknames for the Church of Jesus Christ of Latter-day Saints a "major victory for Satan." I felt like Dr. Zee was always on Kurt's side, that she blamed our problems on me because I'd begun to question church leaders. It also seemed to me that she let him get away with rants she should've called him to task for. He was in the middle of one right now.

"I've spent my whole life being a provider so that you could stay home with our children. And you're happy for me to keep working full-time, saving up for retirement, but you aren't putting in any work on your side. Now that the kids have grown up and left, instead of recommitting to service in the church, you're using all your free time to find things to snipe at and criticize. Why don't you do something productive? Or get a job of your own?" he demanded.

Dr. Zee turned to me. "How does that make you feel, Linda?" she asked.

How did it make me *feel*? It made me want to light Kurt's entire wardrobe on fire—no, to burn down the whole house. It made me want to tear up every family photo we'd ever taken. To call Samuel on his mission in Boston and tell him to come home immediately instead of wasting his time convincing other people to join this church.

In therapy, I was the villain in everything and Kurt was the poor, long-suffering hero who had to put up with a wayward, unrepentant wife. Couldn't he see that this narrative was the problem? The church constantly centering male development and ignoring women? Did he ever try to sit in my point of view, to think about what it had been like to be the one at home with the kids for thirty years, then to have nothing to do and no visible path to make a difference in the church because I had been born the wrong gender?

I took a breath and let it out. Then I tried to find some words that were more constructive. I was trying to be an adult here, even if I was the only one. "It makes me feel sad," I said.

"Would you like to expand on that?" Dr. Zee asked.

No, I would not. And she certainly wouldn't want me to start shouting in here. I breathed in deeply, seeking the sense of spiritual enlightenment that I'd once found so close at hand. "Let me just say that I understand Kurt's frustration. He married me with one set of rules in place, and now I've changed those rules on him."

This was not our first session with Dr. Zee; in fact, we'd already been doing this for a couple of months. Sometimes it felt like we'd never moved past the first session, just circled around the same issues over and over. It was hard for me to tell how much of that was Dr. Zee's fault and how much was Kurt's. Or maybe it was mine, and I just couldn't see it.

"If you wanted this version of feminist equality, you shouldn't have married someone who wanted you to be a homemaker," Kurt said. "I love you, Linda, and I always thought we saw eye to eye, but you can't turn around and say now that you've been oppressed our whole marriage. Raising our children is what you chose—it's what you wanted. And now you're acting like me asking you to do anything that God commands of us makes me a sexist pig."

Another deep breath. This was Kurt's most-used tactic. He turned every complaint I had about the church into a personal attack against him. If I said the institution was patriarchal, he thought I was saying *he* was power hungry. If I said that the leadership didn't listen to concerns about women, it was me implying that *he* was selfish and insensitive. It shouldn't have surprised me, given that the Mormon Church—or, rather, the Church of Jesus Christ of Latter-day Saints—worked very hard to make its members feel that everything in their lives revolved around the institution itself. Work, home, social activities . . . everything should be church related.

I tried again. "I have changed, I'll admit that. I understand that it's difficult for you to figure out what you're supposed to do in response. But I'm not asking you to give up the church, I'm just asking for you to stretch yourself to see things in a more nuanced way, not just in black and white."

I'd talked to Gwen Ferris, a former member of our ward and a dear friend, about the problems in my marriage a little bit over the last few months, but I'd eventually stopped because it was clear she thought the only solution was divorce, which was where she and Brad had ended up. She claimed that there was no such thing as a mixed-faith marriage, just two people who hadn't admitted yet that their marriage was over—or ones who were waiting for their partner to finally come around to their way of thinking.

"That's a lie," Kurt said, his face red. "You're asking me to give up God entirely, to accept your view of Mormonism as a fiction written and perpetuated by Joseph Smith, a man I revere next to Jesus in the work he did to save humanity. He gave his life as a martyr, and you think of him as little more than a con man out for financial gain and sexual excitement with women other than his wife."

He was never like this when we were at home; it was so strange to see this change in personality. I'd have said before we started therapy that he was the gentlest, most even-tempered person you'd ever meet. I hadn't realized the extent of the anger toward me that he'd been swallowing day after day. Now it was all coming out.

It was true that I had mixed feelings about Joseph Smith as a prophet. I did believe he'd been inspired by God in many ways but that polygamy had been nothing more than his own sexual appetite, excused by his supposed revelations. That mistake had not only indirectly led to his assassination but continued to cost the church dearly over the next century and was still causing damage to the women (and men) who had been born into fundamentalist branches and might never find their way out.

But I'd thought this was a topic we'd already discussed and agreed to disagree over. Kurt had known when we'd first gotten married that I wasn't your typical Mormon woman. Even if I'd chosen to stay at home with our kids, I'd always had feminist views. It felt to me like he was the one rewriting history in his victim narrative.

"That's not what I'm asking at all," I insisted. "I'm asking you to accept that other people might see Joseph Smith that way and still find power and truth in parts of Mormonism." Me, for instance.

Dr. Zee opened her mouth to say something, but Kurt cut her off. He'd insisted that he wanted to talk to a female therapist, and I thought it was partly because he found women less intimidating and less judgmental. But also, frankly, because he thought emotions and feelings were women's work, not men's. I don't think he could have respected a male therapist, though of course he would dismiss this as ridiculous if I said it aloud.

"Power and truth? You're talking about my religion like it's just some book you picked up and are considering for an award. Either the church is God's one true religion on Earth or it isn't. Either Christ came and atoned for our sins and was resurrected so that we will all be redeemed or He wasn't. Either the temple seals families together forever in a real heaven that we will go to or it has no power at all and is a fraud," he said, then stopped. He was breathing heavily, sweat starting to drip down his face.

I wasn't the one who'd set up these dichotomies, but I'd certainly heard church leaders frame things this way. It made it easier for them to convince people that any doubts were sins in order to keep them fully invested. Until it stopped working—like it had for me.

"Linda, would you like to respond?" Dr. Zee asked.

On the contrary, I'd have liked to go home, make a half dozen pies and maybe some Christmas candies, and eat them all by myself. But that probably wouldn't save my marriage.

"I don't see the world in those absolutes, Kurt. I believe in so many things within Mormonism, but I'm not going to let church leadership have that kind of power over me any longer. I just can't."

I'd stopped paying tithing in September in protest against the church's reaction to its abuse scandals. This protest made Kurt decide he wouldn't be able to give me a temple recommend as the bishop of our ward. In response to that decision, I'd taken off my temple garments a few weeks ago. Yes, I was being as petty as he was. But I did feel better without the garments on.

"Obedience is the first law of heaven," Kurt said.

Sometimes it seemed like I didn't even need the flesh-and-blood version of my husband anymore. I could just get a cardboard cutout and record a few handy Mormon scriptures in a disapproving voice.

Why was I trying so hard to save our marriage? Maybe Gwen was right.

I was still attending church, though I'd begun to feel freer to simply stand up and walk out of meetings where people said things I couldn't accept. Including sacrament meetings that Kurt presided over and had arranged speakers for.

"Do you really think that God is as anal as you're suggesting He is?" I countered before Dr. Zee could intervene again. "That there's no allowance for any gray area? That He doesn't care about our reasons for supposed sins? Because that hasn't been my experience with God over the years. I believe God is infinitely merciful."

"An infinitely merciful God would lead to absolute chaos. What kind of heaven has no order in it?" Kurt challenged.

Maybe one that extended grace? Another deep breath. How could I have been blind to this all these years? Or had Kurt become more extreme in his stances in response to me drifting away from the church?

"All right, I think that's enough for now. I know you two both have important things you need to say, but I'd like for us to focus on some actions you can take each day this week to feel more connected to each other," Dr. Zee said, holding up John Gottman's *The Seven Principles for Making Marriage Work*, which I'd already read. I hated the oversimplifying the book did, but I dutifully pretended to talk to Kurt about it because that was our assignment.

If I refused to do our homework for the week, it seemed like admitting our marriage was over. And I couldn't bear the thought of telling my five sons, three daughters-in-law, and two grandchildren that Kurt and I were getting a divorce. I couldn't bear telling my ward members I'd given up. And maybe, just maybe, there was a bit of selfish laziness in there, too, because I didn't want to think about moving out of our house, dividing up our assets, and trying to live on my own without Kurt's wise financial stewardship—not to mention his continuing income and investment in retirement. I was too old for all this. As much as I talked about changing the way I saw the world, the truth was, I didn't want things in our marriage to change.

I'd watched Brad and Gwen Ferris go through this over the

last year, and their divorce had made me certain I didn't want anything of the kind. It had become so clinical, so legalistic. They'd had to list every asset and then decide who got what. Brad got the house. Gwen got their savings. Brad got his car. Gwen got hers. The clothes, furniture, even the food storage in their basement. Everything had to be monetized and then fought over.

From my perspective, Brad was the easiest man in the world to get along with, and I suspected he still loved Gwen and was deeply hurt by her decision to end their marriage. He had seemed broken lately, especially after being released from his calling as Kurt's second counselor in the bishopric. He still came to church, attended all his meetings, but he was a ghost of his old self, never speaking, as if being divorced meant he had no longer had any spiritual authority.

I hated what Gwen had done to him and that she was no longer just around when I needed her. She'd moved thirty miles south to the city of Orem, where Utah Valley University was located, so she could finish her classes at The Police Academy there. I had to either drive down there to meet her for lunch between classes or make do with talking to her on the phone or by text messages.

And Anna Torstensen, who had been my best friend for years, had started making excuses not to get together with me. I'd once believed our friendship would survive any hardship, but now I saw the truth. Mormonism was a dividing line, and she was on one side, while I was on the other.

CHAPTER 1

I was returning home from the post office after shipping a package to Samuel for Christmas when my cell phone buzzed. I looked down to see that my oldest son, Joseph, was calling me.

"Hello?" I said.

"Mom, can you talk?" he asked, his voice thin and desperate as I'd never heard it.

"Of course." I always had time for my children.

"I need some advice. Or maybe more than that. There's a young woman missing from our ward up here in Ogden."

"Who is she?"

"Her name is Sabrina Jensen, and she's only fifteen years old. She's been babysitting Carla almost every weekend since she was born. She's a really good kid."

"Do you think she might've run away?" I asked, a few possibilities playing out in my head, from a fight with parents to an Internet romance.

"I don't know," Joseph said. "She disappeared last week, but she didn't leave a note, and her parents say there wasn't a fight of any kind that would trigger something like this. She's so young, and Willow and I are both worried about her."

I felt sick at the thought of a teenager disappearing this close to the holiday season. Out alone in this kind of weather, who knew what could happen? Not so long ago, I might have been content to say a prayer or to add her name to the temple prayer rolls, but "thoughts and prayers" seemed insufficient when it came to helping others now that I didn't believe God answered calls that way.

"Has anyone checked her room to see if she took her wallet or purse or any clothing with her? If she's a minor, they should file a missing persons report with the police." I'd gained enormous respect for the Draper police department in the last few years, especially Detective Gore, who had dealt with me on several cases, calling me out when she had to and always remaining professional. But in Ogden, I had no idea who the investigating detective would be or whether the department would even put a detective on something like this.

"That's one of the problems right now. Her parents don't think it's anything to worry about and are refusing to call the police," Joseph said. "I was wondering if you could come up and talk to them. I'm taking today off from work to stay with Willow and Carla, but it would help us all feel better if we knew you were looking into it."

If Willow was so worried that she wasn't teaching any of her ballet classes, she must have really been shaken up.

"You know I might not be able to do anything, right, Joseph?" I said. I'd poked my nose into a handful of cases in our home ward, but that was it.

"You will, Mom. You actually listen to people," Joseph said.

Kurt would be furious about me involving myself in a situation like this again. Apparently, I was supposed to be busy homemaking, doing my dutiful womanly work without stepping outside of his carefully drawn lines. Well, to hell with that. A missing girl mattered, and I wasn't about to turn my back on someone who needed help.

I sent Kurt a text letting him know I was going to visit Joseph and Willow in Ogden, leaving no room for him to disapprove. If he wanted a say in my decisions, he'd have to learn to support his wife.

I drove up I-15 and turned off on Highway 89 closer to the mountains. Ogden used to be a train depot but was now mostly known for the new temple that had been built over the old one downtown.

As I drove, I tried not to replay various arguments with Kurt in my head, but it was hard. Whenever I was alone and unoccupied, my brain would immediately scratch the same groove in our old record. I knew I shouldn't blame all our problems on him, that I needed to start looking at the ways I was falling into unhealthy patterns, but I couldn't go back to who I'd been just a few years ago, and that was all Kurt seemed to want.

I pulled off just past the canyon and drove up to Joseph and Willow's old '50s brick classic rambler with a lovely view of the valley. They had an incredible backyard with a fountain studded with natural stone.

I knocked on the door, and Joseph let me in. I could see Willow holding Carla on her lap in a wooden rocking chair, though the baby seemed to be asleep. She was just over a year old, and there was a protectiveness in Willow's manner that could be because another mother's daughter had gone missing. I instinctively understood that fierceness. When I had lost my own daughter, Georgia, to stillbirth more than twenty years ago, I had come home and hugged my boys so tightly they squirmed to be let go, and weeks had passed before I could bear to let them outside again.

I thought back to Kurt in those days and found myself softening toward him. He loved his children so much. He loved me, too, even if he didn't like me very much right now. Frankly, I wasn't sure I liked me, either, so I guess I could understand that.

"What can I do to help with this missing girl?" I asked Joseph.

"Her name is Sabrina. Sabrina Jensen," whispered Willow. "She's the sweetest. She takes such good care of Carla. Always tries to make sure the house is cleaner when she leaves than when she gets here, even though I've told her she doesn't have to."

Carla started to stir, and Willow wiped at her face, which was covered with tears.

"She's fifteen," Joseph said. "She always comes to church, but Willow says she doesn't have many friends among the other girls her age."

That wasn't unusual in a Mormon ward. The boundaries were set geographically, which in Utah meant that a few blocks would comprise an entire ward. The idea that you would end up making friends with the people who happened to live in the same three-block radius as you was convenient but not always reality. And the youth were even more isolated than the adults, often separated into smaller groups for church activities based on age.

"Let's sit down for a minute, and you can tell me what you know already," I said.

I pulled Joseph toward the futon and sat on it next to him. He was nearly six-foot-two, the tallest of my sons but also the thinnest. Sometimes I wished I could get him to eat more and fill the hollows in his cheeks.

"Mom, I don't know what to do. I thought that if we all just did what the church taught us, we'd be protected. How does something like this happen?" His gaunt expression made his face look even paler than usual.

I thought about how Georgia's death had changed everything for me. I had ceased to believe in certain promises of Mormonism after that. Kurt was sure our daughter was waiting for us in heaven and would be as long as we were both faithful to our temple covenants and followed all the rules. I wasn't so sure about that. I'd never had the impression that she was still alive somewhere else. To me, she felt profoundly gone. Maybe I'd never gotten over that and my problems with the church now were just the end result of me losing faith back then. I thought I had moved on, but had I really? Maybe all of this was just a distraction from the old grief coming to the surface.

I brought myself back to the present moment when Joseph spoke again, "Sabrina was such a good kid. The best with Carla. She seemed to really enjoy playing with her. She always treated Carla like she was interesting, like she was a puzzle to figure out even if she couldn't speak. To me, she was the kindest, most Christlike of all the kids at church. She wouldn't just leave without saying a thing."

But sometimes the most sensitive and empathetic kids had

the hardest time at church because they couldn't just go along to get along. They called out bad behavior, even if it led to backlash. I played with the theory briefly, then waited to see if there would be supporting evidence. Just like Detective Gore would do.

"Do you think I can speak to Sabrina's parents?" I asked. Some parents knew their children well; others, less so. In Utah, I noticed a common Mormon parenting model based on obedience, punishing teens if they were caught experimenting in some small way, like drinking coffee or getting a tattoo or wearing clothing that wasn't modest enough.

Joseph nodded eagerly. He was probably glad that he could actually do something for Sabrina. "Yes. I've already contacted Sister Jensen. She's willing to see you and let you look around the house, including Sabrina's room. She says she can't tell if Sabrina took anything with her or not, except for her school backpack. That's definitely gone."

He had only mentioned Sister Jensen. "What about her father? Is he not in the picture?"

Joseph looked uncomfortable. "He is, but he's not around much, especially at this time of year."

I put a mental Post-it note on that, to return to later. "So why do you think they don't want to contact the police?"

Joseph made a face. "Sister Jensen says her husband thinks Sabrina will come back on her own in a few days and that he doesn't want her on official record as a runaway."

So he believed she'd left of her own accord. Interesting.

But Joseph clearly didn't believe that. I could almost hear Detective Gore's voice in my head. *Get the evidence first. Put any judgments aside for now.*

"Can you tell me why you think it's not just a runaway situation?" I asked.

"Mom, she's so naïve. Last month, there was a combined Young Men/Young Women's lesson about dangers of the Internet, and she kept saying that people online weren't any more dangerous than people in real life. What if someone lured her out to a rendezvous of some kind?"

Clearly, the police needed to be notified. But I would have to talk to her parents about that. "All right. Let's go see her mother," I said, standing up and motioning toward the door.

"We can walk. They live just down the street," Joseph said.

I followed as he went out the door and started walking downhill.

"How long have you known this young woman?" I asked.

"Three years. Since we moved into the house. But she's been babysitting for us since Carla was born, so we've gotten closer to her recently."

I nodded and walked down the hill with him. We arrived a couple of minutes later. The brick house was built in a '70s ranch style with what I'd call white "wings" on either side of the dark-brown brick center section.

Joseph knocked at the heavy wooden door in front. It was answered by a dark-haired woman who looked like she couldn't possibly be five feet tall. Her hands were tiny, and if it weren't for the small wrinkles around her eyes, I would have thought she was a child.

"Mom, this is Sister Jensen."

"Rae," she said, shaking my hand gently.

"And you can call me Linda," I said as she gestured me inside.

"Nice to meet you. My husband is at work today," she explained. "He runs a Christmas lighting business, so it's one of the busiest times of the year for him."

"Of course," I murmured. Joseph's comment made sense now. I wondered how he supported the family the rest of the year. Or did Rae Jensen work as well? I had to stop assuming everyone adopted the same roles Kurt and I did. Maybe what I really needed to combat my sense of powerlessness in Mormonism was to get a job.

"I told her she could take a look at Sabrina's room," Joseph said, gesturing farther inside the house.

"Before we do that, could we talk for a few minutes?" I interrupted. "I'd like to better understand Sabrina as a person before I see her things. They'll mean more to me."

We sat in the living room, which was filled with holiday knickknacks and festooned with red and green garlands, though I didn't see a tree up yet. There was a family photo with Sabrina, but it must have been taken a few years ago. She looked just out of her preteen years and had a big smile on her face, her arms wrapped around both her parents.

"What would you like to know about her?" asked Rae, who refused to sit even though she gestured me and Joseph to the couch. Her hands folded repeatedly over each other in nervous habit.

"She's such a good babysitter. Carla is so happy with her, and I know that's not easy," Joseph put in, breaking the ice, smiling.

"I've always told her she was a little mother since the moment she was born," added Rae, her face lighting up suddenly. "The way she used to line up all her dolls in rows, giving them little kisses and taking care of their every need."

She was idealizing Sabrina, which I didn't think would help us to find her. "Can you tell me about her relationship with you? And her father?" I asked.

"Oh. Well, she's our only child," Rae said. "Clint always doted on her, and she on him. Little daddy's girl." I couldn't tell if that was jealousy or just wistfulness in her expression. "She used to help with the lights in the winter. And the summer lawn business. But she's been too busy lately."

"When did she get too busy?" I asked, thinking that she'd had the time to babysit for Willow and Joseph.

Rae waved a hand. "Just this year, I suppose. She leaves early to catch the bus to school, then comes home and stays in her room. Says she's studying. We hardly talk to her at all."

Alarm bells began to go off in my head. "Did you ask her if something was wrong?" I asked.

"Well, since the big blowup, we haven't talked much," Rae said.

Aha. "When was that?" Maybe this would all be solved in a day or two and things would go back to normal.

"In October, I think. Her father tried to talk to her about pulling more weight around the house. You know, if she wasn't going to help with the business, then he thought she should be doing chores. Cleaning the house. Doing dishes. Making dinner once or twice a week."

"But she didn't want to do that?" Joseph was the one who asked this, clearly confused since she'd seemed eager to do those tasks at his house.

"She said that nothing she ever did was good enough for us. And then she said that we shouldn't have had children if we"—Rae choked up at this, and Joseph reached over to put a hand on her shoulder until she got out the second part—"if we'd just wanted an obedient Mormon slave."

A strange accusation. Was Sabrina Jensen being an unreasonable teen, or was there more going on behind the scenes with her parents?

Time to change the subject. "Could you tell me the names of Sabrina's friends? I can ask them if they have any ideas of where she might have gone," I suggested. They might be willing to tell me more than her parents would.

"Well, there's Cheleigh. And Kindra. And Lexie," Rae said, counting them off like she'd known I was going to ask.

"And Bailey," added Joseph.

"Are they all members of the church?" I asked.

"Yes, of course," Rae said, straightening up as if I'd insulted her. "All good girls."

"Does Sabrina have any friends who aren't Mormon?" I asked. Mormons were taught to be friendly to non-Mormons from an early age, but there were boundaries. As long as you were showing those outsiders how good the church was, it could count as missionary work. But too close a friendship with someone outside the church could eventually lead a good Mormon away from "the one true church," away from God and the celestial kingdom.

There was only silence from Rae, so Joseph stepped in. "Sabrina mentioned another young woman named Bella a couple of times," he said. "At our house." There was a kind of apology in his eyes as he looked at her.

Rae frowned. "Yes, Bella. I told her to break off that friendship. But she wouldn't listen to me. I don't like Bella at all.

She's a wild thing. And she's always with that boy, Henry whatever his name is."

At least I was getting some real information. Detective Gore would have been able to push harder as part of an official investigation, but I had to get what I needed more quietly.

"Henry and Bella," I repeated, thinking that Sabrina might feel more able to share whatever parts of herself to them that she might not feel safe showing her parents or other Mormons. "Can I have their phone numbers?"

Rae gave me their numbers, as well as the ones for Cheleigh, Kindra, Lexie, and Bailey, plus the numbers of two boys she said Sabrina had seemed to have crushes on a few months before, Peyton and Jonathan.

"Of course, she isn't dating yet. She's only fifteen," Rae assured me.

Sixteen was the official starting age for dating within Mormonism, though plenty of parents looked the other way or made excuses for "group dates" or for school dances that they didn't want their children to miss out on. Once, I'd have been judgmental about those breaking the rules, but I was learning to see how rigid that way of thinking was. Were the rules really to protect the children involved, as Kurt would have argued, or was it all about the way it made parents look to other Mormons?

"Mom?" Joseph nudged me.

"Oh. I'd like to talk to her father, too," I said.

Rae gave me his number as well. "But he can't answer while he's working. He's up on rooftops and it's not safe, so he doesn't even carry his phone with him."

That seemed sensible to me, but the man's whole attitude

about his daughter going missing seemed off to me, carrying on with work as if nothing was wrong.

"Let's see her room, then," I said.

"Of course." Rae stood up too quickly and nearly fell over. Joseph caught her and helped her upstairs.

CHAPTER 2

Sabrina's bedroom, when Rae opened the door, was not at all what I'd expected. It was so tidy. Not at all teenager-like. There were no posters on the walls, no clothes on the floor, no certificates of achievement or even textbooks that I could see.

There was a copy of the church youth magazine, *The New Era*, on Sabrina's nightstand, but it didn't look like it had been opened. Her scriptures, with her name in silver on blue leather, were on top of her dresser. A copy of *The Miracle of Forgiveness* by Spencer W. Kimball, the prophet of the church in the 1970s, was in a small bookcase. Samuel had told me what he thought of that book and what it had to say about "the sin" of homosexuality—that it was better to be dead than to be homosexual—but Kurt had loved it when he was a teenager and found it very hopeful and healing.

"Does she have a cell phone?" I asked. I glanced around the room long enough to catch sight of the tail of a cord attached to the charging brick on the wall.

"An iPhone," Rae said.

"Have you tried calling it?"

"Dozens of times, but there's no answer."

"Would you mind trying again?" I asked.

As she did, I waited for any sound in the room.

Silence.

I bent down and checked under the bed, then glanced around the carpet in the rest of the room. I checked the dresser drawers briefly and then the nightstand. No phone. Not surprising that she'd taken it—teens always had their phones with them these days.

"Wait. Where's her sleeping bag?" Rae said, bending down next to the bed, where I had just been. "And the pad for it."

"She had a sleeping bag and pad under her bed?"

"She used to go on camping trips with her dad." Another brief flicker of that jealous-wistful expression on her face. "She knows how to take care of herself." She glanced around the room, but there was no sign that the items were still here in the room. Sabrina had taken them with her.

Self-reliance was a core value of Mormonism, and we started to teach it at a young age, but should that apply to a fifteen-year-old girl living outside on her own in the middle of winter? Not in my book.

I was frustrated by Rae Jensen's lack of panic over what seemed like a potentially dangerous situation. I tried to accept that maybe it was just shock or the same sense of helplessness I sometimes felt as a Mormon woman who had no power in our church's structures.

"When was the last time you saw Sabrina?" I asked. Detective Gore always went for a timeline first.

"I don't know," Rae said, looking aimlessly about the room as if she might find the answer somewhere on the white walls.

I looked at Joseph.

He said, "She was supposed to babysit for us on Friday night. When she didn't show up, I called Rae to see if anything was wrong. She told me then only that Sabrina hadn't come home from school that day. But when we talked later, on Saturday, Rae, you said Sabrina hadn't been home on Thursday after school, either, isn't that right?"

"Well, I don't know," Rae said, still looking away from me. "I was out shopping on Thursday afternoon, so it's possible she came home after school and left immediately afterward. But she didn't sleep at in her bed that night. I know that much."

There was something else that she didn't want to tell me. We'd have to get there slowly. "When did you get home on Thursday?" I asked.

"About six P.M. I was worried about getting dinner started so late," Rae said.

"And your husband was working all day Thursday? Did he see Sabrina in the afternoon?" I wished he were here so I could at least get a read on him.

"No, he was out past midnight that night. I didn't even have the chance to tell him Sabrina was missing until Saturday afternoon. He was angry that he had to do the jobs alone again since she'd flittered off without a word like a spoiled teenage brat." She put a hand to her mouth as soon as she said the last part, aware of how it must have sounded to me and Joseph.

So it was more than just the blowup. There were problems here. Parental expectations set too high. Was it more than that?

"Why didn't you call the police when she first went

missing?" I asked again. The question was awkward, even accusatory, but my inner Detective Gore demanded I ask it. I turned to Rae, whose shoulders were stiff, and held her gaze.

Rae shifted to one foot, then the other. "I'm sure she's fine. Probably with friends, having fun and not thinking about anyone but herself."

Such harsh judgment—was it hers or her husband's? "Is she normally a selfish girl?" I asked. That wasn't the impression I'd gotten from Joseph at all.

"Well, you know how teenagers are these days. They watch YouTube and Netflix and do those chats with other kids on the Internet without thinking about their family or church obligations. They think they have rights, that they're owed something."

I glanced at Joseph, whose lips were pressed tightly together. "She was a great kid. Well-mannered, kind, attentive to Carla," he said.

Rae flinched at this. "Well, she's a good actress. She always puts on her best self for other people."

I thought about the church books and magazines on Sabrina's shelf and again wondered if she'd ever felt like she could be herself at home. But, even so, that didn't seem like enough motivation to leave home in winter. There was more going on behind the scenes. I would have to start with her friends. Maybe there were some more forgiving parents who had offered her a place to stay and assumed Sabrina would tell her parents where she was. That was the simple answer to all of this.

Except for the fact that she had taken her sleeping bag and pad.

"Has she ever disappeared like this before?" I asked.

"No, never," Rae assured me earnestly.

"So you saw her Thursday morning when she left for school?" I asked.

"Yes," Rae said.

"And how did she seem?" I asked. "Anxious? Distracted? Upset?"

"She left before I was really awake," Rae admitted. "I just nodded to her as she went out the door."

Not helpful. "What about on Wednesday night? Did anything unusual happen then?" I asked

"Not that I recall," Rae said, moving toward the door. "She came home. We had dinner. She said she had homework. Then she went to bed."

I stifled a sigh of frustration. "Did she talk to any of her friends that night?" I asked.

"I don't know," Rae said with a shrug, her hand already on the doorknob.

I took one last look around the room, my last chance to catch something. I was keenly aware that I had no formal training as a detective—all I saw was a very clean room, and I wondered what I was missing. "Has she always been this tidy?" I asked desperately.

"Actually, no," Rae said, eyes widening in surprise. "How did you know that?"

Relief washed over me at this one small crumb that Rae seemed willing to talk about. "When did she start cleaning up so much?"

A contemplative tilt of the head. "Maybe two or three months ago?" Rae said. "I don't know what happened, but I came home one day and found her on the floor, packing things into bags to toss or give away. She cleaned all the furniture with polish and even used our special shampooing vacuum on the carpet. She pulled down everything on the walls—all her favorite posters and framed certificates."

"You didn't ask why?" I said, trying not to sound judgmental. Something big must have happened, and I suspected it was bad.

She opened the bedroom door. "Sabrina said she was just tired of living in a dump," she said dismissively. "Frankly, I was relieved. I was tired of threatening her with sending her father in with garbage bags to throw everything away if she didn't pick it up."

I turned back to the bed, which was made as neatly as if it were in a hotel room, corners perfect and the blue floral bedspread smoothed out without a single wrinkle. What kind of teenager was so careful about these kinds of details?

Rae stared at me impatiently as I stepped away from the bed and opened the closet. Inside, the clothing was neatly divided into thirds. Dresses on the left, skirts in the middle, and blouses on right. They were color coordinated in a gradient from white to yellow, orange, pink, red, purple, blue, green, brown, and finally black. I could see a just few gaps where clothing seemed to be missing. It was chilling to me somehow, this level of perfect organization.

As we walked down the stairs and toward the front door, I thought about how to get anyone to talk to me, especially Sabrina's non-Mormon friends, Henry and Bella.

But before we left, Rae added one last thing. "I think she'd put on weight. She started wearing bulkier sweaters, long sleeves all the time, even when it was warm. Hats, too, and sometimes gloves."

What? No one had mentioned this before. I looked at Joseph.

"I didn't notice any weight gain," he said, frowning.

"Was she eating more? Or different foods?" I asked.

"If anything, I thought she was eating less. But that isn't possible, is it? You can't gain weight unless you're eating more," Rae said.

"She didn't eat much at our house, either," Joseph put in. "We always bought treats for her, but she never touched them, as far as I know."

None of this seemed like good news.

"Do you think you can find her?" Rae said, a pleading tone in her voice, though she wasn't looking at me directly.

"You really should call the police," I advised frankly.

Rae just shook her head. She opened the front door, waiting for us to step out.

"We'll find her, Sister Jensen. I promise," Joseph said in my place, though I sincerely wished he hadn't.

Then we headed out the front door.

CHAPTER 3

Joseph and I headed down the driveway. "Now I want to know what worried you about Sabrina before she disappeared," I said. He wouldn't have called me if he hadn't noticed something before all this. He'd have gone along with her father, saying she'd come home eventually.

Joseph went silent for a while. We walked up toward the mountain in the dark. Finally, he said softly, "A few weeks ago, she asked me if I thought anyone would want to marry a slut."

"What?" How horrible. "How did you respond?"

He shifted uncomfortably. "I asked her if she wanted to talk to me about why she thought that word applied to her, but she turned red and shook her head. I didn't press the issue. I figured it wasn't my business. But I was worried about it. And then this happened."

"You think she was sexually active?" I said. It wouldn't be so unusual for a fifteen-year-old, even in Mormon Utah.

"I don't have any other reason to suspect anything. I didn't want to bring it up with her mother, of course. Even that just seemed like a random conversation at the time."

So that was what he'd been holding back, probably to

protect Sabrina's image—or her parents'. "Well, thank you for telling me now. At least I have a couple of starting points. And I won't tell anyone about that conversation." Sabrina had clearly trusted Joseph enough to ask him that question, and I didn't want to betray either of them or risk harming her reputation.

When we got back to Joseph's house, Willow was in the front room, her hair wet from a shower. Carla had been put back to bed, it seemed, though Willow would start at even the smallest sound, as if she expected it might be her own daughter being kidnapped from the nursery.

"How are you?" I asked.

"On edge," she said plainly, rubbing at her eyes, which only made them redder.

"Sit down," Joseph said. "You need to let yourself rest."

I sat next to her, patting her arm. "I agree. We're going to find her, so don't worry," I reassured. "Did you . . . notice anything unusual with Sabrina before all this?"

Willow's eyes flickered up to Joseph's.

"Go on," he said softly.

"Well, the last few months, I thought she might have some kind of eating disorder," Willow said. "I tried to talk to her about it."

"And?" I prompted.

"She said it was none of my business—that her body was her own." Willow's hands were turning around each other like they were working dough.

Of course her body was her own, even if you'd never hear that in church. Women who showed their shoulders or stomachs were "walking pornography," according to certain church leaders.

"Did you ask if someone said something to her?" I asked.

Willow shook her head. "I just let it go. She was right. It wasn't my business. But still, that's what she would say if it *was* a problem. So I waited for another moment to talk to her. And now she's gone."

There were clearly several changes in Sabrina that had happened in the last few months. Her room becoming spotless but devoid of anything personal. Her blowout argument with her father about work and chores. Her change in clothing choices. And her question to Joseph.

"Did she ever talk to you about a boyfriend? Or a boy she was interested in?" I asked, thinking back to the names her mother had given me. Henry, Peyton, Jonathan. She'd had a crush on both Peyton and Jonathan, according to her mother, but I was most curious about the only non-Mormon, Henry, who could have had different rules for dating.

Willow chewed on her lower lip. "She talked about one young man in the ward a lot a few months ago. But at some point, I realized it must have gone wrong."

"Peyton? Jonathan?" Joseph asked.

She snapped her fingers. "Jonathan, I think! But then she stopped talking about him all of a sudden. She went rigid when I brought him up a few weeks later."

"Hmm," Joseph said.

"So they never dated?" I asked.

"Not that I knew of," Willow said. She started silently crying again. Finally, she said, "Sabrina asked if I thought the church could ever be a place for someone who wasn't the perfect Mormon they talk about in lessons. I wasn't sure what she meant, but I told her about Samuel being openly gay on his mission. I told her that the church is for sinners, not saints."

I went quiet at the mention of Samuel. Things hadn't been easy for my youngest son, and I wouldn't have cited him as a model for a "sinner" or the "imperfect" Mormon, but if Willow had thought it might help Sabrina, I understood.

It sounded more and more like things were adding up to premarital sex, which was supposed to be equally enforced on young men and women but never was. Young women were thought of as temptresses and constantly told they had to be the ones to say no, because the church needed young men to go on missions and later serve as priesthood leaders. They would run the church, and the women would work behind the scenes.

Willow wiped her tears and took a shuddering breath. "Sabrina said she hoped nothing bad happened to Samuel. That he should have kept the truth to himself so people couldn't hurt him."

I let out a sigh. "I'll have to talk to more people. See if anyone else has a lead." But I would also have to be careful not to dispense more information than I got. Detective Gore was always so good at that.

"I feel so guilty about all of this," Willow said as I stood up.

"What do you mean?"

"I don't know. I feel like I should've acted earlier, when I first wondered if something was off. I should've tried harder to get her to talk to us. I thought she trusted us. That she knew we could be relied on in a situation like this," Willow said.

What situation was that? I wondered.

"What if something like this happens to Carla when she's

older? What if she runs away one day and we have no idea why?" Willow added, her hands shaking.

It occurred to me that Willow needed some serious time to herself. She was stretched so thin with work and the new baby. I made a note to myself that I should talk to Kurt and see what we could do to help. That was perhaps the only thing Kurt and I never argued about: helping the kids.

"I'll talk to you later," I said and motioned for Joseph to follow me out the door.

"So what do you think? What's my next step here?" Joseph said. He had always been a doer. If I gave him a list, it would be finished by the end of the day. But if I expected him to spot a need on his own, he struggled more.

I was tempted to tell him to make sure Willow had more time to herself so she didn't burn out or become resentful, but I didn't want to interfere. It was his marriage, not mine. I would come back when I had help to offer, like babysitting on a more frequent basis.

I turned the focus back to Sabrina. "As of now, I think she left on her own. But why? And why now? The fact that she has a sleeping bag makes me worry that she's on the street, not with friends. That sounds so lonely—and dangerous."

I shivered as I said it, despite my heavy coat with gloves and a wool hat in the pockets if I wanted them.

"Do you have a photo of her that I can borrow?"

"I don't know, maybe." He took out his phone and started thumbing through it. "Ah," he said after a moment, and he held up a cell phone picture of her with Carla. It wasn't high quality, but it was clearly the girl I'd seen in the family photo in Sabrina's home: medium height, boxy clothes, with a slightly twisted tooth on her left side, and brown hair to her shoulders.

"I'll send it to you," he said. "Let me just crop Carla out and zoom in on Sabrina."

I nodded, thinking about that pale, thin face.

"Look, maybe I'll head into the mountains tonight to see if I can find any sign of her there," Joseph said. "I know some of the spots where she went camping with her dad. Last year, anyway."

I thought about Carla and Willow alone at night without him. "You should go during the day, while it's still light. And warm."

He nodded. "All right. But we'll talk as soon as either of us has new information?"

"Good plan," I said. I hoped Sabrina was staying at a friend's but feared she might have joined the increasingly large population of teens in Utah who had walked out of or been thrown out of their Mormon homes due to conflicts with their parents' religious ideals or who had come to reside on the street because it was safer than life at home.

There were few places that would take in teens, some of whom had their own problems accepting authority, from what I understood. But I didn't know much about living on the streets. I'd never had a reason to find out. My life had always been privileged, as had my sons'.

CHAPTER 4

As I drove south from Ogden into Salt Lake City toward our house, I couldn't stop thinking about Sabrina Jensen. There were so many homeless teens downtown, I figured I could drive by and ask if anyone had seen her. I'd texted Kurt that I was heading home, but I could plead traffic if this delayed me enough for him to notice.

As soon as I turned past North Salt Lake with its refinery, I could see the Capitol Building to the north of the rest of downtown Salt Lake, up above the Avenues. It was small in comparison to the handful of skyscrapers we had, but it was even more visible set starkly against them. The temple, which was right in the middle of the circle of new high-rises, wasn't as lucky. Unless you were right in front of it, you could easily miss the crown jewel of Brigham Young's years as autocratic leader of the Mormon Church. It was an impressive piece of architecture, especially when you considered the destitute circumstances of those who'd built it largely by hand.

I took the downtown 400 South exit and drove around Temple Square, lit up for Christmas in stark contrast to the streets surrounding it, where a good portion of the city's poorest population lived. It was dim enough under the clouds that I could see the brightly colored lights wrapped around the tree trunks and spreading into the branches.

The temple itself was always lit up with golden light, Christmas or no Christmas, but even under reconstruction now, the grounds were green and red and blue. Then there was the reflecting pool across from the temple, right where there used to be a road connecting the downtown area with the rest of the city. The church had bought the entire property, road included, in the '90s, stirring up quite a controversy. But people rarely talked about it that way nowadays. It was just a lovely place to go during the holidays, and if traffic was a little more difficult downtown, you got used to it.

The reflecting pool bridged the iconic Salt Lake City temple and the church office building next to it, as well as the Lion House, which was renowned as the main residence of Brigham Young and the favorites of his fifty-five wives (though the church missionaries who led tours there tried to downplay this aspect).

I'd told myself I was just going to park and observe from the car, but all the spots were full, so I drove beneath City Creek, the lavish domed, multimillion-dollar investment of the corporate LDS Church. As I came up from the massive underground parking structure, I couldn't help but feel a bit of a glow at the timed dance of the water fountains and the happy faces of the children dressed in warm hats, standing with parents and watching excitedly. I turned away from this and toward Temple Square, keeping my eyes out for any vulnerable-looking teenagers about Sabrina's age, especially in a group.

It had been four days since Sabrina Jensen's mother had last seen her. However difficult it was living on the street, half a week wasn't enough for her appearance to have changed beyond recognition, surely. I fixed the image of her medium-brown hair and eyes and that one slightly crooked tooth in my mind, trying to focus on that instead of the bitter cold or the shoppers passing by. It was impossible to look closely at every face, and Sabrina almost certainly wouldn't be shopping, so I ignored everyone with bags and didn't bother trying to find her among the giggling groups of teenage girls with steaming hot chocolate in their hands, headed to the lights on Temple Square.

If I were Sabrina Jensen, where would I go?

There were plenty of adults in worn clothing begging on the edges of City Creek asking for money from typically well-to-do shoppers. I checked my purse for my wad of dollar bills, which I kept on hand specifically for any trips downtown. Kurt thought pulling out cash in public was foolish and warned me that I was asking for attention from "the wrong people."

"We have an obligation to help the poor," I had argued to Kurt.

"We have an obligation to help the poor *who turn to God*," Kurt would say back to me. But to me, this was following a different rule from the Book of Mormon. We weren't supposed to judge people who asked for help, just to give. It was one of the most difficult of God's commandments.

I kept replaying arguments like this with Kurt in my head, even though I knew it wasn't helping my marriage.

Living my own morality, I handed a dollar bill to the first

person holding a cardboard sign past Temple Square. This first sign read: STRANDED IN UTAH AND WANT TO GET HOME FOR THE HOLIDAYS.

"God bless you," said the woman in response. I suspected that this was something she had learned to say specifically to Mormons.

The next sign read, DYING OF CANCER. THANKS FOR YOUR SUPPORT. I gave a dollar to the man holding it and received a simple "Thank you." He was skeletal and certainly looked like he was near death, but he also smelled strongly of alcohol.

Again I reminded myself to refrain from judging. And if he wasn't a Mormon, he didn't consider drinking a sin.

There were humorously honest signs like the one I passed next, which read, DON'T I DESERVE A HOT TODDY FOR CHRISTMAS, TOO?

"Hot damn, thank you, ma'am," was the response to my dollar there. The one dollar wouldn't buy him a hot toddy all on its own, I told myself to counter my reflexive guilt.

I knew that Utah boasted one of the country's most compassionate government programs for the homeless, Housing First, which helped people pay a portion of their housing by getting them social security and other government funds without setting conditions like getting clean or taking mental health medication. But minors couldn't be helped under this program, and I suspected Sabrina Jensen wouldn't know how to ask on her own. If she was really here and not just staying with a friend in Ogden.

No longer worrying about the time, I reached the corner near the Salt Palace and turned left. I passed by Abravanel Hall, the home of the Utah Symphony. Then I saw a handful of young people with signs and decided to take a chance. There was a group of four dressed in low-waisted jeans, double hoodies with the strings pulled right, and gloves and jackets over that. The clothing looked worn and smelled unwashed, and I found myself already starting to breathe through my mouth rather than my nose in anticipation of the smell, feeling a twinge of shame for my prejudice.

I put my ones back in my purse and got out a twenty instead, holding the bill in my hand as I walked toward them. They might have heard about Sabrina or known someone who'd met her. I spotted one young man in a heavy coat with a kind face.

I began with, "Hello. I'm looking for a fifteen-year-old girl. I'm worried about her." I didn't say anything about how I knew her. I held up my hand at about her diminutive height. "About this tall. Brown hair, brown eyes. Crooked tooth in front."

I reached into my pocket, fumbling for my phone with cold fingers. "I have a photo, if you want to see it."

"What's her name?" asked one of the girls nearby, walking over. I got a quick glimpse of her face, angular and frowning, with bruises under her eyes and one on her jawline. Her clothing was quite threadbare, probably from several months of wear.

"It's Sabrina—"

Before I could say her last name, the girl grabbed the twenty and started running.

"Wait!" I called out, but she was already out of sight. I sighed, but at least it was only twenty dollars and I hadn't pulled my phone out. What had I expected in wandering here? To miraculously come across Sabrina within minutes?

I stood back upright and realized how suddenly the girl had approached us on my describing Sabrina's appearance. I wondered whether it had been that or just the money.

I thought about texting Kurt but decided against it. Given the terms we were already on, it would only make him angry. I would have to be more creative if I stayed here to ask around. That had been my only twenty, and I was no closer to finding Sabrina.

I looked up and wrapped my arms around myself. It wasn't nighttime yet, but the clouds had turned the sky dark, and I didn't know if snow was coming. I glanced down the walkway in the center of the lower level of the Gateway and caught a glimpse of a group of teens with backpacks and sleeping bags. I headed in their direction; they were standing under one of the overhangs by the steps to the second level, and they looked up at me suspiciously.

For a moment, I was sure I saw Sabrina Jensen. The girl was small and had brown hair that was the right length, and while I couldn't see her face well enough to check for her telltale crooked tooth, I could see she was carrying an overstuffed backpack and something bulky under one arm. But that was all I saw of her before she disappeared—I didn't know where.

Desperate, I glanced around, trying to figure out where she might have gone. Up the steps? She couldn't have gotten up them so fast, could she?

"Sabrina!" I shouted, despite my resolution not to call out her name again. I chased down the walkway, looking both ways as I went, but there was no sign of her. "Sabrina Jensen!" I called out again, though by then I was breathing so hard that her name came out garbled and labored.

I closed my eyes and tried to fix in my mind the image of the girl I'd seen. Then I opened my eyes again and got out my phone to compare with the photo of Sabrina Jensen. Was it really the same young woman? It might have been.

It could also have been someone else completely, whom I'd frightened with my loud voice. These young people faced risks I probably couldn't understand. It was one thing to be homeless as an adult. It was another to be so young on the street—at this age, they were especially vulnerable to sexual assault and trafficking.

I walked back to the steps, where the rest of the group stood hanging around, eyeing me carefully. They didn't seem to want money, and of all the eyes I had met today, these were the most pained. What in their young lives had brought them here? What were their stories?

I made one last cursory search of the mall and the Front-Runner station by the North Temple bridge. There were plenty of people there, sitting against the advertisements, lying down on the benches underneath the canopies. I didn't see anyone who looked like Sabrina, but it was entirely possible she was there and I was missing her.

It was past seven o'clock, and I was freezing. I resigned myself to going home and thinking of a better plan to find Sabrina.

I made my way back to the car, only remembering to call Joseph once I'd already paid for my parking and was headed toward the freeway. I told him about my possible spotting of Sabrina downtown.

"What? Really? Are you sure?" said Joseph.

"No," I admitted. "No, I'm not. I only caught a glimpse before she ran away."

"But you think you saw her? How did she look? Was she okay?" asked Joseph.

"I really don't know if it was her." Now I was regretting the call. What if I'd been completely mistaken? "I didn't see her for long enough."

A frustrated exhalation. "What are the chances you think it was her?" he asked.

"I can't say," I said.

Before exploring this further, I had to talk to the friends of Sabrina's whose information Rae had given me and find out what had triggered her obsessive cleaning and her change in eating habits before she'd run away. I needed to understand who Sabrina Jensen was, what she needed, and how far she'd go to get it.

"All right. I'll call you tomorrow, and we can talk about what to do next," Joseph said.

"I love you," I said, and hung up.

CHAPTER 5

I stopped for some burgers on the way home. By the time I got there, I was two hours late for dinner. It looked like Kurt had taken out his laptop and worked while he was waiting. I noted to myself that he hadn't called for a pizza or tried his own hand at making dinner. He'd waited for the burgers that I brought home, nearly cold.

We ate at the counter because, these days, it didn't seem worth it to set the whole table for just us two. It was Monday night, which meant we'd usually do Family Home Evening, but with the boys all out of the house and what had happened in therapy today, I wasn't sure I wanted to spend time with my husband trying to make conversation—or hear him lecture me on his theme of black-and-white obedience within Mormonism.

"How about we watch some TV?" I asked.

"All right," he said.

So we sat on the couch, watching the latest crime show. It was far too violent and reminded me of Sabrina again. Kurt received a call halfway through the episode and went into his office for almost half an hour. Someone in the ward, presumably.

"What's going on? Who's calling on a Monday?" I asked when he came back for the ending. I was curious, I'll admit, but also worried. Monday was sacrosanct in the church. No meetings, no activities. Only family time.

"I can't talk about it, Linda. You know that," he said, giving me that look that said that I was supposed to accept his word because he was our bishop and my husband, and that was how things were.

But it was annoying, and more than that, it seemed intended to make me feel small and unimportant. Was this retaliation for what happened in therapy, or was this just what our marriage had become?

No wonder I'd jumped at the chance to look for Sabrina. Some problems were easier to solve than others.

KURT WAS OUT of the house early the next morning. I had the feeling it had something to do with his phone call the night before, but again, he didn't say anything. I let it go. Which was convenient, since I had my own plans for the day. Maybe this was how our marriage would look in the future: separate lives in the same house, a distant civility, and shared fond memories.

It wasn't how I'd imagined our senior years. I'd always thought we'd serve together in the church, be one of those couples who went on multiple missions together to foreign countries, but I didn't want that anymore. The idea of letting church leadership tell me where to go, how to spend my time down to the minutest detail, always knowing that next year, they might decide what I had done wasn't fruitful enough and start from scratch with someone else's plan—I couldn't do that. I needed more control over my own life, my own soul.

But I could look for Sabrina Jensen, and I could support my son Samuel with whatever came after his mission. I could be a Mama Dragon and try to make other Mormons see that the church wasn't Christlike enough when it came to LGBT issues. And if at some point I couldn't do that inside the church anymore, I would find other ways to be an activist. Maybe that would become my new religion, helping people on the margins and trying to change the world for the better.

I didn't think phone calls would be useful in the morning when Sabrina's friends were at school, so I did some quick laundry and vacuuming, then hurried to run a couple of errands, including taking Kurt's suits to the cleaners. He had several suits now, and I tried to ignore the annoyance I felt that it was my job to make sure they were clean. I was still living on his income, after all, and I wasn't interested in getting a job other than the one I had as a general busybody, part-time savior, and full-time mom to whichever of my sons needed me.

After lunch, I called the number I had for Sabrina's father. He didn't answer, probably still asleep after working on Christmas lights late last night. But I left a message and asked him to contact me as soon as he could.

I got in the shower, and when I got out, my phone was ringing. I saw from the number that it was Mr. Jensen calling me back. I threw a robe on and picked it up before the chance was gone. "Hello, Sister Wallheim."

"This is Clint Jensen, Sabrina's father."

"I'm so glad you called back," I said brightly. "I'm Joseph's mother, from your ward. You know that Sabrina babysat for him a few times? For my granddaughter, Carla?"

"Yes, of course," he said in a hearty tone. "So how can I help you? You have some lights that need to be put up? It's a little late, but I might be able to squeeze you into my schedule."

His accent was pretty rough, with dropped *r*'s and hard *g*'s everywhere. From that, I guessed he'd grown up on a farm somewhere in northern Utah or Idaho, which was never an easy job with the short growing season and problems with soil. Not to mention the lack of water in our desert climate.

My father had been born on a farm in southern Idaho, and he'd told me about what it was like, the hours of backbreaking labor and dwindling pay. He got out of the business when he'd finally earned his college degree, but that accent stayed with him his whole life.

"No, I'm not calling about Christmas lights," I said. How could he ask me that when his daughter was missing?

"I can give you a great deal. I'm working round the clock to make people happy," he offered.

"Actually, I wanted to talk about Sabrina. Her disappearance," I said.

A beat, and then, "Oh, I'm sure she's just off having fun. I'm sorry if she's worried you." He sounded annoyed.

I tried to explain my line of thinking. "I don't think she's just staying with a friend. Did you notice that she took her sleeping bag?"

He tsked. "We tried to raise her right, her mother and I. We taught her right from wrong. I thought she was a good kid. But then she starts backtalking and thinking she knows more about everything than her elders. She questions everything, uses bad language—makes me think about God and the third of the host of heaven."

He was referring to the spirit children of God who followed Lucifer rather than Christ in the premortal life and were cast out, unable to gain mortal bodies. The story came up frequently with Mormon parents who wanted to justify themselves when it came to children's bad choices. After all, God lost a third of His children, too. And He hadn't been a bad parent.

"It sounds like Sabrina has been having some problems just in the last few months. Any idea what might have happened to change her behavior?" I tried to ask casually, but I didn't quite think I was managing it.

His response was immediate. "Well, it wasn't anything that my wife or I did, if that's what you're thinking. She has friends of her own, stirring up ideas in her head. Making her imagine that she doesn't have to follow our rules anymore. We put our foot down, but we had every right to do that. Any good Mormon parent would do the same."

I was tired of beating around the bush. "Your wife said you had a fight with her in October. Did you threaten to kick her out or give her the impression she wasn't welcome at home anymore?"

It was the wrong tack.

"That is none of your business, Mrs. Wallheim," he said in a sharp tone. "And I don't take kindly to your interference. If you don't have anything more useful to offer, I'll be going back to my work now."

Damn. I had to try one last time. "I'm just worried about your daughter," I said. "I'm sorry if I'm pressing too hard. My son is worried about her, and I want her to come home. Don't you?"

"Of course I do," he said. "You're not with the police, are you? Or some kind of private detective?"

"No," I said. It was too difficult to explain my history investigating disappearances and other crimes without explicit help or permission from the police. So I continued: "Joseph just thought I could help because I'm a mother, too. And a member of the church." As soon as I said it, I realized I should've used Kurt's status as bishop to bolster my authority, as much as I hated doing so.

He sniffed. "Well, Sabrina can come home anytime she wants. But that doesn't mean she won't have to obey our rules and think about someone other than herself for a change."

"I'm sorry if she's disappointed you." I tried sympathy to smooth things over and see if that would get him to open up. I wished I could see his facial expression.

Ranting now, he said, "She wants to blame us for everything instead of looking in the mirror. That's where she sees a victim, instead of someone who needs to buck up and fly right."

Victim. That was telling.

I was sure Sabrina Jensen had faced a trauma great enough for her to run away, and her parents both knew something. I wasn't sure what it was, but she was alone in the middle of winter, a thought I couldn't stand.

After some comforting murmurs of agreement, I said, "I'd like to talk in person to get more of your perspective on your daughter. If I understand her problems, it could help me figure out where she's gone."

"She's got plenty of problems, that's for sure," he said.

I breathed a tiny sigh of relief at getting him to open up,

even if it was just to vent about his daughter. "When would you be available?" I asked.

"Sorry, but I'm booked solid until January," he said with a sigh. "I've only got a few hours of sleep scheduled a night. That's part of the reason I haven't been chasing after Sabrina myself."

"Maybe I could meet you at one of your job sites?" I suggested.

A huff of laughter at that. "No, not a chance. Our insurance costs are already out of control; there's no way I can afford to have a stranger there. I'm sorry, but I think you're out of luck."

"Well, thank you anyway," I said and hung up, feeling completely useless.

CHAPTER 6

I looked up the names and numbers of Sabrina's friends that Rae Jensen had given me. I needed the kind of information about her that only friends would have. How much they'd tell me depended on my approach. It was usually adults I had to convince to spill their secrets. But with teenagers, it wasn't as simple as bringing them home-made bread and cookies—or was it? My boys had always been hungry. Their teenage girlfriends had been trickier, but some of them liked homemade goodies. What did I have to lose?

I had until school got out that afternoon to make some-thing, so I got out the favorite that my boys had always asked me for growing up: fudge-walnut-coconut bars. I did the crust first, with chopped walnuts, butter, sugar, and flour. I pushed half of the crust into my cookie sheet, reserving the rest to dot the top of the chewy center.

Then I cooked the crust as I worked on the stove. First, chocolate chips melted, then sweetened condensed milk, and finally, a whole bag of shredded coconut. When the crust was finished, I poured on the chocolate mixture, then put on the top crust to make a kind of homemade sandwich cookie—leagues above any Oreo.

I'd made this recipe for every potluck I was ever asked to bring a dessert to and never brought home a single bar. I let the pan cool before I cut my creation into pieces.

I went online to try to find family names or addresses for the cell phone numbers I'd been given. Sadly, nothing came up, maybe because I wasn't familiar enough with online searches. If Samuel had been here, I was sure he could have made the Internet spit out the proper information. I was stuck with calling Rae Jensen and asking her as nicely as I could if she could give the addresses to me.

She hemmed and hawed while I gently told her I was fine with waiting while she looked things up. *No, no need to call me back. I'll just wait. No problem. I'm taking a break anyway.*

Finally, I had addresses for Cheleigh, Kindra, Jonathan, and Peyton, which Rae must have gotten from the ward's online database. She said she would see if she could find the others. Four was better than none, so I thanked her and asked her if she remembered anything else from just before Sabrina left.

"If there's anyone I'm concerned about in her life, it's that boy Henry," Rae said.

I'd had a similar thought earlier. "Was she dating Henry?" I asked.

"No, of course not. She was only fifteen," she insisted.

Which didn't mean anything. I told Rae again that I'd do what I could and hung up. Signs were pointing to some romantic involvement Sabrina had had before she'd left. I wondered how I would be able to convince her that she had nothing to be ashamed of, that her parents would welcome her home, no matter what she did—or continued to do.

I started to think about a temporary place for her to stay while we figured this out. If I did find her, there were Encircle houses in Salt Lake and Provo, but that was mostly for LGBT teens. Maybe Youth Futures in Ogden? They took in kids who needed a place to stay for any reason, but that was so close to home, which she might not want.

Find her first, I told myself. *Then you can figure out how to help her.*

Finally, a couple of hours later in the car with the bars packed in sealed plastic containers, I headed to the first address, Cheleigh's. I arrived at the street address and sat in my car, waiting for the school bus.

Sure enough, the bus arrived in a few minutes, and I could see a young woman who had to be Cheleigh walk into the house. She was dressed in ballet flats, which seemed ridiculous to me in this chilly weather, and she didn't have a coat or hat or gloves on. Her pale skin was blotched with red cold spots, and her long hair was braided demurely down to her waist, dancing as she walked. She was wearing a long-sleeved lacey top and jeans, and she hugged herself tightly as she hustled into her house.

I knocked on the door a few minutes after she'd gone in. A minute passed before a face appeared in the window. I waved and held out the goodies, hoping she would assume I was a new Young Women's leader in the ward coming to introduce herself.

She opened the door. "Hi?" she said.

"Cheleigh?" I said.

"Yes?"

I held the fudge bars out as a kind of card. "My name is Linda Wallheim. I brought you some treats." Was I going to let her assume she should know me from the ward? I could tell by the way she was scrutinizing me—trying not to come off as rude while doing so—that she thought I looked familiar. I did have that kind of face.

"Uh, thanks," she said as she took the bars, poking at them with interest.

"Go ahead, try one. You just got home from school. I'll bet you're hungry."

With zero suspicion or fear of negative consequences, she put one of the bars to her mouth, made a moan of joy, and stepped back into the house, leaving the door open for me. I worried that she wasn't a bit more careful, though it had worked to my advantage.

I stepped inside and closed the door.

"I heard you were friends with Sabrina Jensen," I said as I seated myself on the couch in the front room.

On the walls were all the requisite Mormon family offerings: photos of the new Ogden temple, of the First Presidency, and of the family (apparently, Cheleigh had a younger brother, who looked about eight years old). There was a painting of Christ—the one of Him in the red robe—and copies of "The Living Christ" and "The Family Proclamation" printed and decorated with smaller images of the family at various stages.

"Sabrina?" said Cheleigh. "I guess. Are you going to ask me to try to fellowship her or something?" She didn't sound very happy at the idea of having to take friendly action toward

Sabrina, which told me something about their relationship—or lack thereof.

"I've heard she's missing. I was wondering if you had any idea what might have happened to her or a reason she might have left home." There it was, honest and open.

Cheleigh put down the nearly eaten fudge bar. "I don't know anything." She put up her fudge-covered hands. "I swear. We weren't very good friends, and we've hardly talked since school started in August."

"And why is that?" I asked. I'd suspected I wouldn't get much firsthand information about Sabrina, but at this point, even gossip might help.

Cheleigh made a disgusted face, her eye twitching slightly. "Well, she was . . . loose. She was dating two guys at the same time even though she wasn't sixteen yet, and it seemed really unfair to me."

"Peyton and Jonathan?" I asked. Rae Jensen had mentioned Sabrina having a crush on both of them, but had she really dated them at the same time? I struggled again not to judge. No matter how much I complained about Mormonism, I was still very Mormon at heart—and not always in ways I liked.

"That was before," Cheleigh said.

"Before what?" I asked.

"They both broke up with her. She said she wouldn't pick one of them over the other. They kept pressing her to decide, but she wouldn't."

That sounded to me like the plot of a young adult novel. "Why not?"

"If you ask me, it was a power play. She liked having both of them dance on her strings, competing for her. And if she picked one, she would have lost half that attention." Cheleigh took the last bite of the bar but seemed to like it less than before.

"That must have backfired on her," I said suggestively.

A snort. "I'll say. They dumped her hard. At the same time. Everyone heard about it. She ran away crying to the bathroom and didn't come out for, like, three periods, until one of the teachers went in to get her."

"I see. And that was how long ago?" This all seemed like old news to Cheleigh, but Sabrina's disappearance was so recent.

A shrug. "It was back in October, so a couple of months ago, I guess."

That timeline didn't make sense—why would she have waited two months to run away?

"Why do you think she only disappeared now? And have you seen her in the last week, by any chance?" I knew I was stretching it since they weren't close, but it seemed worth asking.

Cheleigh shook her head, looking slightly guilty now. "Like I said, we don't talk much anymore. I know that sounds un-Christlike of me, but I guess I'm just worried about her being a bad influence."

Right, because *that* was what Christ was always so worried about. He said to stay away from the publicans and the prostitutes because they might be a bad influence.

I took a deep breath and asked, "Do you remember the last time you saw her?"

"I don't know. I guess last Wednesday at school." It was almost a question. "She was crying, and she looked awful. Snot streaming down her face, her makeup all messed up, clothes on wrong."

Crying at school the day before she'd disappeared? This had to have been the catalyst to her disappearance.

"At school?" I echoed, my mind racing through the possibilities. Probably not a fight with her family, then. "What do you think happened there?"

"No one I knew bothered with her anymore. Maybe she was just PMSing," said Cheleigh.

Great. When girls dismissed their own gender so readily because of hormones, that was not a good thing.

"Anything else you can think of?" I asked. "About Sabrina having problems at school or in the ward."

Cheleigh shook her head.

A dead end. I switched gears, even though I knew the answer to my next question. "Was Sabrina popular at school? Or in the ward?" I hoped she wouldn't think I should already know this as a local Young Women's leader.

She made a choking sound. "Uh, no. Not after the thing with Peyton and Jonathan. No one would talk to her anymore. None of the real people."

"Real people?" As opposed to fake people?

"Mormons, I mean. You know." She waved a hand.

I loathed this way of looking at the world, but I had to admit it was prevalent among Mormons. And I was still one of them, which I supposed meant this trait of seeing "us" versus "them" was as much my problem as Cheleigh's. Sometimes I thought it just made it easier to keep people scared enough to stay in, no matter what their problems were. Other times, I thought it was about strengthening community ties.

"What about Henry?" I asked. "Her mother mentioned him.

Did Sabrina date him, too?" If they'd broken up afterward as well, it could explain her crying at school.

"Henry?" Cheleigh giggled. "No way."

"Why are you so sure?"

"If you ever saw Henry, you'd understand. He's, like, two feet tall. And gay."

"Oh," I said.

"Sabrina only hung out with him because he was a reject, too. So was that girl Bella."

Ah. I took a deep breath and sighed at the subconscious implication that Mormon Church was more of a social club than a religion. As a teenager, it was easy to look at things this way and assume some people just weren't "good enough" to get in.

"So Sabrina wasn't dating anyone when she left?" I was nearing the end of my patience with this girl's narrow-minded outlook, but at least we were almost done.

"No. No one wanted anything to do with her," Cheleigh said. "We all knew she was a bad influence, like I said." She hesitated and then added, leaning in to me, "I saw her buying a pregnancy test at the store. She was carrying it in a bag, but I could read the label through the plastic. She said it was for Bella, but why should I believe that?"

In silence, I considered the implications of the pregnancy test, which might not have been for Bella.

After a moment, I stood up. "Well, thank you." I wasn't sure there was anything to thank her for, though. I didn't follow this up with *See you later*. I hoped never to have to speak to this girl again but reminded myself she was a child, still under the influence of her parents, teachers, and peers.

It was them I should be angry with. And maybe even myself, for participating in the system that taught her these beliefs.

I fumed in the car for a few minutes and ate one of my own fudge bars, debated for a while about having the rest, and decided against it.

I drove to the next address on my list and knocked on the door. Kindra opened it, and I introduced myself again with the container of remaining fudge bars held out prominently, a smile on my face, bishop's-wife mode on full sparkle.

She let me in, and I explained to her that I was worried about Sabrina Jensen.

"Did you know she was missing?" I asked.

"I heard. I mean, I noticed she wasn't at school, but I thought maybe she was just sick. Or, you know, depressed or something."

"Do you know if she was being bullied at school?" I asked, trying a different tack than with Cheleigh. "I'm trying to figure out why she would run away."

"Well, no one called her names or pushed her or anything." Kindra shifted on the couch, looking uncomfortable. Her long blonde hair was in perfect curls that spilled over her pink crocheted sweater. I was pretty sure she hadn't made the sweater herself, although crocheting was a skill you couldn't have gotten through Young Women's without learning when I'd been her age. How times had changed.

"What did they do to her, then?" It seemed like she was skirting the issue.

She shrugged nonchalantly. "I don't know. Mostly ignored her, I guess. Silent treatment stuff. But she really deserved it. She didn't follow the rules, you know."

In addition to the more explicit age restriction for dating, there were a number of unspoken rules within Mormonism for young women: wait until you're asked on a date, only date one boy at a time, wear attractive but not immodest clothing, do what you're told by leadership, do well in school and don't brag about it, never ask for more than you're given. I knew the rules all too well, and for once in my life, I was glad I didn't have a daughter who had to negotiate a place amidst them.

"Was Sabrina afraid of anyone that you knew of?" I asked, not expecting much.

To my surprise, she said, "Actually, yeah, I guess. She avoided certain people, you know? She would see them and immediately turn around and walk away. Sometimes she'd get red in the face and start shaking. Once, she even ran into the bathroom and threw up."

All this new information about Sabrina complicated the picture of her in my head. I hoped this peer bullying wasn't connected to her calling herself a "slut" or the pregnancy test she'd bought.

"Can you tell me which people scared her?" I asked.

Kindra hesitated but proceeded to answer. I silently cheered for the lack of boundaries that Mormonism encouraged, especially for young women talking to adults. "Well, Peyton and Jonathan, but some of their friends, too." She looked away.

"All right, thank you," I said. I'd heard enough about Peyton and Jonathan that I knew I needed to talk to them. I had their addresses from Rae but asked Kindra if she knew Henry's and Bella's.

She pulled out a paper copy of the school handbook and showed me their information in the listing. I was surprised to discover they lived next door to each other. I said goodbye and headed out to speak to them, only because I wasn't sure I was ready to ask Peyton and Jonathan the right questions just yet. I wanted to make sure I had enough answers first.

CHAPTER 7

After wandering around for a few minutes, unsure about the street numbers, I parked in one of the older neighborhoods in Ogden. The houses here had larger lawns than other parts of the city, but they were less well-cared-for. The brick was old and crumbling on some of them, and many had tacked-on additions that didn't look up to code. I wasn't there long before I realized that most of the residents weren't speaking English to each other—and that I stood out like a sore thumb.

Thankfully, I didn't have to embarrass myself by knocking on a door and attempting to communicate in Spanish because in a few minutes, a young Hispanic woman walked by in tight jeans with decorative holes in the thighs. Next to her was a half-Asian teenage male with a streak of red in his hair whom I suspected was Henry, based on his height and Cheleigh's earlier description.

I stepped in front of them and held out the container of fudge bars. No need to pretend I was a Young Women's leader here. "Hi, Bella and Henry. My name is Linda Wallheim, and I'd like to talk to both of you about Sabrina Jensen," I said directly.

If I'd had any doubt about their identity, their reaction to Sabrina's name was all the confirmation I needed. Henry flinched and looked around, as if for a place to hide. Bella's face grew coldly inanimate.

"Who's Sabrina to you?" she demanded.

"A family friend," I said, despite the fact that I'd never met her. It wasn't exactly a lie, since she'd babysat my grand-daughter.

"So?" she said.

Henry was still looking up and down the street as if he suspected I'd brought backup.

"Sabrina is missing, and I wondered if you had any thoughts on what might have caused her to leave home," I said.

Bella kept her lips tightly shut and shook her head. Well, she definitely wasn't Mormon. This kind of closedness wasn't part of our culture, but I admired it, regardless of how inconvenient it was for me in the moment.

Henry looked at me, eyes narrowed. "Why should we talk to you?" he asked.

"I'm trying to help Sabrina," I said impatiently.

"Right, by making her come home when she hates it there?" he asked.

"No," I said. "Not if she feels she can't stay with her parents. But I'm trying to find out what happened before she left. I need to know what was so terrible at home or at school that she'd choose to run away."

If any of my suspicions about the toxic environment of these two places to Sabrina were wrong, it didn't show on the faces of these two.

"We shouldn't talk here," said Bella.

"Can I take you out for something to eat?" I asked, wishing we had a better place to chat than the middle of the sidewalk. Neither of them was inviting me into their homes, and I wasn't going to push it. But I wanted a comfortable place to try to convince them they could trust me.

"You can't bribe us with food, you know," Bella lashed out, staring down at the container of fudge bars, which I now wished I'd left in the car. "It's not like we're going hungry."

"I just meant I wanted to find a place we could talk in private instead of out here," I said.

They looked at each other. They seemed worried enough about Sabrina to consider it, which said something to me. Cheleigh had only worried about herself.

"Is that your car?" asked Bella, nodding to it.

I said yes, and she and Henry headed toward it, opening the back doors without a word. I got in, then reached back and put down the container of fudge bars on the central armrest, which seemed to be the key. After a moment, Bella held it up and offered one to Henry. Soon, they were both chewing after all.

"You don't know about what happened to Sabrina," Bella said slowly.

I shook my head.

Bella glanced at Henry.

"Those boys. They did something to her. It was so awful, I don't even know how to—" She stared out the window, fuming, as if strangling them in her thoughts.

"Jonathan and Peyton?" I guessed.

She nodded.

It felt like I was close to finding out about the explosion

that must have rocked Sabrina's life, based on the debris left behind. Her parents had sensed it, too, even if they didn't know exactly what had happened. I had to brace myself for the truth. I said cautiously, "I heard they broke up with her because she wouldn't choose between them."

Bella shook her head and popped the last bite of the fudge bar into her mouth. When she was finished chewing, she said, "It's what they did after they broke up with her."

She eyed another fudge bar but didn't take it. Henry was on his third. He ate a lot for his size, as hungry as my boys had been in high school.

I felt sick to my stomach, every muscle in my body tense. But I had to know, however bad this was. I waited in silence.

Finally, Bella continued, "They were so mad at her, even though she never lied to either of them. She was always open about seeing both of them—only in groups—and told them she wouldn't choose between them or officially date either of them. She didn't want to get serious because she was so young."

So she'd followed the Mormon rule book, despite what her parents and church friends might have thought. "If she made that clear, why did they keep pursuing her?" I asked.

To my surprise, it was Henry who answered. "It was a game for them," he said. "Don't you think?" He reached a hand out and placed it gently on Bella's shoulder.

She nodded but didn't speak. There were no tears in her eyes, only sparks of ice.

"They treated it like a competition, scoring points against each other. And maybe Sabrina was flattered by the attention at the first. She just didn't realize the consequences," Bella said.

The consequences? This seemed to go beyond the scope of making two boys mad. I was dripping with sweat and rolled down the window despite the cold outside.

"You think she's a slut, too, don't you?" said Bella. She reached for the door handle.

"No, of course not," I said, realizing she had misinterpreted my reaction.

"What they did to her—" said Bella. "They're monsters. She was just trying to be true to herself. Making sure they didn't just see her as some prize."

"What did they do?" My voice was raspy, but I was begging, not demanding.

"They . . . they raped her," Henry said quietly between gritted teeth.

"Peyton and Jonathan raped her?" I asked, just to be sure. The same two "good Mormon boys" in Joseph and Willow's ward?

Henry nodded.

"Not just them," hissed Bella. I turned to her and could see her fingernails digging into the gaps in her jeans, making red marks on her skin.

"Who else?" I asked, feeling as though I had just been thrown into a stormy ocean, about to be swallowed by a whale.

"They got their friends together. Ten or twelve of them. She didn't know how many. She said she didn't even remember their faces after the first part, after Peyton and Jonathan. But they held her down for the rest. As long as she could still fight and even after she gave up." She got the words out, but she was choking on them by the end, crying now.

I felt tears sting my eyes and hated how useless they were because Sabrina was still out there in need of help. There was no time for anything but anger, which would speed me up instead of slowing down the search.

Bella and Henry didn't say anything for a while, and no one was chewing anymore. The silence was palpable.

In the end, it was Bella who broke it. "You going to tell us we're wrong, aren't you? That they wouldn't do anything like that. 'Cause they're good Mormon boys," she said bitterly.

Good Mormon boys. The phrase was sickening to me right now. Had Sabrina said that to Bella? Had someone said it to her when she tried to tell them about the assault?

I shook my head. It was the only motion I could manage without risking vomiting.

"She said they told her it was what she wanted. That since she didn't choose one of them, she must have wanted all of them. They called her a slut and a whore who had asked for it. And she told me she wasn't sure when they were finished with her if they were right. I want to see them suffer for everything but especially for that. Convincing her it was her fault," said Bella, her words so flat it broke my heart.

"When?" I finally got out.

Bella shook her head. "When what?" she asked.

"She's asking when it happened," Henry said.

Bella shook her head, as if the timing couldn't possibly matter, as if pain like that was eternal. And maybe it was.

"It was in October. The beginning of it, I think," Henry said. "I don't know the exact day. She didn't start hanging out with us until a couple of weeks later. I think for a while she was pretending to go to school but she just spent all day in the bathroom, trying to avoid those guys."

I was speechless and horrified; I tried to distract myself by struggling to figure out the timeline. If this had taken place in early October, why had she waited two months to leave home?

"I tried to talk her into going to the hospital or a rape counseling center. It was too late for a rape kit by the time she told us," Bella went on.

"Why didn't she tell her parents?" I asked, though I suspected I already knew.

"Her parents?" Bella's tone dripped with disdain. "All they care about is whether she makes them look good. They want control over everything in her life. If she takes a single step out of line, then anything that happens is her fault."

I couldn't rightfully defend the Jensens from this, based on what I'd seen and heard so far. Some parents were like this. They had children because it was expected and because they wanted, if not a "slave," as Sabrina had accused them of, then a puppet they could dress up and parade around at parties to make themselves look good. Even if they didn't really try to connect with or understand that child.

"But why did she only run away a few days ago?" I asked.

"She was terrified they would do it again," said Bella, slapping her hands on her knees so loudly it must have hurt. "That's what they kept telling her."

This was getting more and more nightmarish. "Peyton and Jonathan were threatening her?"

"Every day," Bella spat out. Then she raised a finger. "But never in public. Never when anyone else was in sight. They were smart about it. Never left any physical evidence. But she was always terrified one or more of them would show up somewhere she didn't expect. At her house, if her parents were gone. At church, if she was alone in a room. At the grocery store. In the bathroom at school. Or out by the bus stop. Or the gym. A million different places. She was going crazy, thinking of all the places they might find her."

So the fear had built and built for weeks.

I thought about the timeline of Sabrina cleaning up her room and wondered if she been trying to make every part of her life—of herself—so perfect that nothing like that would happen to her again. No wonder she'd started that conversation with Joseph. This explained the oversized clothing, even with her eating less.

Oh, Sabrina.

I wished I could see her in front of me and give her a big hug. Tell her it wasn't her fault. There were so many people who had failed her.

"Have you told any other adults about this?" I asked Bella. Surely there was someone equipped to deal with situations like this, someone in a far more official capacity than me. The police? Or at least a school counselor?

"We tried to get her to," said Bella. "But Sabrina was too scared."

Gang-raped. In Utah. By a group of Mormon boys. And she'd had no one to help her deal with it except two friends who knew little more than she did about the world.

It was too much. I'd held in my worry and shock for too long. Now they were flooding out. I scrambled for the car door and vomited onto the blacktop outside. I wished I hadn't had only those fudge bars for lunch. They tasted terrible coming back up.

I closed the door again and looked back at the two teens. For the first time, they seemed to take me seriously, staring with wide eyes. Who knew throwing up was a great trick for interrogations? I supposed it made me look human, vulnerable. If only I could do it on command. But I doubted it would impress Detective Gore.

"She won't want to go back home," I said, thinking out loud. Even if her parents weren't as bad as Henry and Bella thought, it was clear she didn't trust them to protect her, and at least two of her rapists lived within a few blocks of her house. The most anonymous place within reach for her would have been Salt Lake City.

"But she shouldn't be on the streets," I went on. She was so young. I needed to help her. To save her. Of all the young missing and suffering women I'd felt bound to in the past few years, she seemed the most innocent.

"There are worse places," Bella said with a knowing look at Henry.

It made sense that they were so cynical. After all, what had happened to Sabrina had been while she was at living at home in safe, suburban Mormon Utah. The juxtaposition was obscene. All the temples, all the statues and paintings of Jesus. All the books about choosing the right path. And this was what had happened.

I glanced back and forth between them. There was still something hidden here; I was sure of it. "Have you seen her?" I asked. "Since she ran away?"

No response from either of them, though both looked away from me.

I said urgently, "I'm only trying to help her. It's not safe for her out there alone." Even if what had happened to her was one of the worst horrors I could imagine, something like it could happen to her again out there.

"She has her phone," Henry said finally. "She calls us sometimes."

Good. Instead of lecturing him about his obligation to call the police, I asked a practical question. "How does she charge it? I know she left her charger at home."

A shrug. "She bought a new one. She goes to the big Salt Lake City Library when she has a chance," Bella said. "It's warm inside, and she can sleep there during the day without getting harassed by the police. And charge her phone. As long as her parents keep paying for her cell service, that is."

How long would that be? Maybe as long as her father could pretend she was just staying at a friend's house.

"Have you seen her in person?" I asked, not trying to seem overly eager.

Please, God, let them trust me enough to tell me the truth.

"We met up with her yesterday. Downtown, near the library," Henry said softly. Henry, not Bella because Bella still wasn't sure about me yet. "She texted us an address."

"And?" I asked.

"She didn't look so good," Henry admitted.

Which was probably why he'd decided to tell me all this, thank God.

"She's gonna be pissed at us, Henry," Bella said. "We promised her we wouldn't tell anyone."

"She needs help, Bella. You know that," Henry replied.

"Tell me what was wrong," I said because it had to have

been bad enough for him to worry. Had Sabrina been beaten up? Was she out of food?

This time, it was Bella who answered. "She looked like she hadn't slept in a week. And her clothes were filthy."

"And smelly," Henry added.

Bella nodded. "She took all the food we offered her and ate it right there. I've never seen her eat so much so fast."

But at least she wasn't in immediate physical danger.

"If I called her number, do you think she'd answer?" I asked.

"She has most numbers blocked," Henry said. "She won't answer a call from anyone she doesn't know."

This was more information than I'd ever thought I'd get. And all I had to do was head to the Salt Lake City Main Library while it was still daylight to see if I could find her. Seemed easier than wandering around downtown again, although this new information made me fairly sure it was her I'd seen last night.

I thanked the two teens and offered them the rest of the fudge bars. They accepted as they got out of the car.

I drove away, knowing that Kurt would definitely not endorse my current plan for where Sabrina Jensen should live if I found her, now that it was clear she wouldn't want to go back home. She needed somewhere safe, and there was only one way to make sure that happened.

CHAPTER 8

What Detective Gore would tell me to do at this point was call the police and report everything Henry and Bella had said. Then I could step back and let them investigate. They would figure out if charges could be pressed. They would find Sabrina living on the streets and bring her back home.

Except that she didn't want to go home. And there was no proof of anything Henry and Bella had said. I was a witness twice removed, and even if either Henry or Bella were willing to speak on the record, their third-person testimony might not even be enough to bring Peyton and Jonathan, the only two whose names we had, in for questioning.

No rape kit.

No DNA.

No statement from Sabrina.

Eyewitnesses? As far as I could tell from that story, only the young men and Sabrina had been present.

If I involved the police right now, I would be setting something in motion that was bound to end in false hopes and ruined reputations—at best. There could be countercharges of slander. Sabrina would be dragged through the mud, possibly into a court case she couldn't win. She'd left home to avoid all that, it seemed, and I couldn't blame her.

I knew what the statistics on rape convictions were in Utah, and that wasn't even when it came to "good Mormon boys." If this had happened in Draper, I could talk to Detective Gore personally, but it hadn't, and I had no particular reason to trust the police here in Ogden.

For most of my teenage years, I'd followed the Catholic Church clergy sex abuse scandals and congratulated myself that we Mormons didn't have to deal with that. But we were a smaller denomination that was of less national interest, so it just took longer for our scandals to come out. Mormons pretended the difference was that Catholic clergy had to be celibate, but the truth was that rape was about power, not sex. And there was plenty of power to be abused in Mormonism.

I wished I could talk to Kurt about this, but I couldn't. I hated that I didn't trust him to be on my side—or Sabrina's. He might well say that I was exaggerating the problem, that we didn't know what the other side of this was or even that my vendetta against patriarchy in the church was getting in the way of me seeing clearly. If I'd trusted him, I could have asked him to call Sabrina's bishop himself and use his authority to get the other bishop to listen.

This was what our marriage had come to. I had to hide the truth from him. And there was a set of things I couldn't do on my own, too. Like call Sabrina's bishop myself. Because I couldn't let it slip that Henry and Bella knew where Sabrina was or at least might be found. Even if he knew the scope of the problem, he would almost certainly just call the hotline number for the church's lawyers, who would tell him to give the boys a slap on the wrist and speak for them if the police investigated.

Boys will be boys, after all. Wouldn't want to ruin their lives, their chances of going on missions in the future. The patriarchal Mormon Church needed men for all those leadership positions that women couldn't fill since we weren't granted the priesthood. If every accused rapist was harshly disciplined, who would pass the Sacrament or do any of the jobs that young men were supposed to do? I could hear the bitter sarcasm in my head as I thought this and wondered when I had become so cynical. What I'd learned today could certainly have been the tipping point.

I drove to Joseph's house instead because I had to talk to my son about this. Sabrina certainly hadn't told him any of this, but as a respected member of the ward, he could help her cause and provide insight.

But he wasn't home from work yet. Willow and Carla weren't there, either. I called him on the phone while standing on his doorstep.

"What is it, Mom?" he said.

"I need you to come home right now," I said.

"What? Why? Did you find Sabrina?"

"No, but I know what happened. I need to talk to you."

Joseph must know these boys. In my mind, there was something rotten at the core of Mormonism if they had been coming to church each week, going through the motions of the priesthood after what they'd done. What about the presumed discernment of the leadership, who were supposed to know when people sinned? Had no one noticed a change in them? In Sabrina?

He sighed. "Mom, I already took Monday off. I can't just leave in the middle of work day."

"*Now*," I said through gritted teeth.

A pause, and then he said, "I'll see what I can do." He hung up.

Climbing back in my car to stay warm, I hoped that Willow and Carla would be away for this. I didn't want my daughter-in-law to have to hear about the horrifying crime committed against her best babysitter, not to mention the young men who had faced no punishment for it. I could take Joseph out for a walk in private, but it was bitterly cold, the wind just starting to howl.

In that moment, I imagined briefly what this weather was doing to Sabrina Jensen, who had only a sleeping bag to protect her.

Joseph arrived about thirty minutes later, waved me to the kitchen with him, and made some hot cider. Not the good kind from juice and real spices simmering in a bag but from a powdered packet. Still, in that moment, it tasted like heaven.

I sipped at it, warming my hands on the big mug that was supposed to look like Santa Claus climbing down a chimney.

"So what's so urgent?" he asked.

I looked at him, only a few years older than the young men I was about to accuse of rape, and pictured in a terrifying moment what I would have said six years ago if someone had told me one of my sons had been a part of something like this. Would I have believed them? Or would I have defended him? I wasn't sure I liked the answer that rose in my mind—of course it couldn't have been one of my sons. My sons weren't like that. I'd taught them to respect girls and women.

"I found out why Sabrina ran away from home," I finally got out. I didn't tell him the part about her charging her phone at the library. I didn't want Joseph trying to contact her directly, not yet. He was too close to the problem and might scare her away.

"Yes, what is it?" He sounded annoyed at me drawing this out.

"I was talking to some friends of hers, Henry and Bella," I started slowly.

"The non-Mormon ones? The ones her mother doesn't like? Do they have something to do with this?"

So easy to blame things on non-Mormons. It made us feel safer.

But I thought of the Mountain Meadows Massacre, a part of Mormon history that had remained covered up for a long time. More than a hundred non-Mormon settlers in a wagon train had been slaughtered, including children, by members of the church who believed they were doing their duty to God. The remains of those bodies had been hidden, and the story had spread that it was Indians who had attacked them. For nearly a century, most Mormons believed this story, until the evidence became just too strong to deny. We Mormons liked to think of ourselves as the persecuted ones, but we'd been the bad guys plenty of times, too.

I had to just say it. "Joseph, Sabrina was gang-raped."

Joseph jerked in his chair for a moment, and then he stood and his eyes met mine. "What? How? By who?"

"Apparently, it happened at school. Henry and Bella told me about it. They said Peyton and Jonathan were the instigators. They were angry she wouldn't date one of them and decided to teach her a lesson. Or something. They cornered her. Called her a slut while it was happening. Said she had asked for it, that she deserved it." I choked on the words.

There was a long, uncomfortable silence, both of us breathing hard.

"I know Peyton and Jonathan," Joseph said then, in shock. "They're stalwarts, Mom. In leadership positions."

"I thought they might be," I said. I couldn't go to the police without evidence, but with Joseph at my side, I might be able to convince those two boys to confess.

"Peyton and Jonathan?" Joseph shook his head. "I just can't believe it. They're such good Mormon boys."

Did he have to use those exact words? "I was hoping maybe you'd be willing to come and talk to them with me. Get them to confess. For the sake of their souls," I said breathlessly. This plan had been percolating in my mind for an hour or more, but I hadn't expected for it to come out like this.

I don't know what I'd hoped for. But when Joseph shook his head, I saw that the church was the same to him as it was to Kurt. Maybe all Mormon men would defend it to the bitter end because they'd been taught that the power of the institution was God's power. They'd been taught obedience, that they would benefit from it. Which they did.

Joseph looked sick. "No, Mom. You can't ask me to do that. I teach their Sunday School class. I know them, what they're capable of. It isn't this."

My fists tightened. He'd asked me to come here to help find Sabrina, not to keep him blind to the spiritual rot at the heart of his own ward. I wasn't going to coddle him.

"What about Sabrina?" I said sharply. "You knew her, too. Aren't you as concerned about what she's gone through?"

He took a breath, then met my gaze. "Fine, maybe they did do something inappropriate."

Inappropriate? That made rape sound like a misunderstanding. There was no question of consent here, and even if the Mormon Church did a terrible job of teaching the importance of that, none of these boys could simply have misunderstood how wrong what they had done to Sabrina was. Neither should my son.

He went on, "Let's think about this rationally." Just like Kurt, he was using that word as a bludgeon, my own equally valid reasoning being dismissed as too emotional. "They have no reason to tell us the truth, even if we go over to talk to them."

"No reason other than clearing their conscience and trying to make things right with God. Isn't that what confession is for? To heal your soul?" I braced for Joseph to tell me that it only worked that way if you confessed to the proper authority, your bishop. That I didn't count because I didn't have the priesthood, nor did the police in their official role.

He nodded. "Eventually, but it sounds like this is recent. I don't know if they'll feel their sins weighing on them yet," he said.

Two months later? More excuses, I thought. "Then we need to help them feel that weight," I said. "And make sure that they give the full list of names to the police."

Now Joseph's eyes widened. "If you think they're going to give us a list of names of other young men involved, that's crazy. Why would they rat out all their friends?"

Because it's the right thing to do? But he was right on one count. Young men this age were very much invested in their reputation with their peers.

Then Joseph said, "Unless you think you can convince them somehow that if they give you a list they won't be prosecuted. That they can turn state's witness or something like that?" He looked at me vaguely, as if I knew which lies to say to convince them.

It was actually a good idea. I wasn't going to make any false promises, but if we hinted at the idea of the police needing a witness to the crime to testify against the others, one of them might break. We had to try. While Sabrina was out in the cold, this seemed the only thing that I could really do to help her. Until we made sure she could live without fear, I had no right to pretend to offer her safety.

"I need you to call them. I want to talk to them tonight, before I go home," I demanded.

Joseph hesitated but, to his credit, only for a moment. Then he nodded. "All right, Mom." And he picked up his phone.

While he was still talking, Willow came home with Carla, all bundled up in her car seat. She had an adorable snowsuit on, one with cat ears and little paws on her feet and hands. All I wanted was to take her home with me and offer to babysit for days on end, relaxing and taking care of her at home. But I couldn't—not yet.

"Were you out shopping?" I asked. "Do you need help bringing things in from the car?"

"If you promise not to peek inside the bags. There are gifts in there," Willow said.

I told her I wouldn't look and unloaded the backseat. From the logos on the bags, it looked like they were mostly for Carla, who wouldn't remember the surprises inside. I remembered when Kurt and I had celebrated our first Christmas with baby

Adam and how he'd loved tearing off the wrapping paper, not caring what was inside at all.

"Okay, Mom, I've set up a couple of visits. We can drive over to Jonathan's first," Joseph said when I got back inside.

"Oh, I thought you were going to stay for dinner," Willow said, looking disappointed. "I figured your mom would be up for some Thai takeout."

I had a love-hate relationship with Thai food. I loved the flavors but couldn't stand the heat, and I got constant teasing from my sons on that point, since they all took after Kurt or had burned off their taste buds on Scout campouts by now.

"Save some for me. I'll eat it when I get back," Joseph said. "Mom?"

"I don't think so tonight. Sorry," I said. I'd never been less hungry, and I suspected talking to these boys would do nothing to improve my appetite. If anything, I'd be lucky to keep everything down.

I walked to the front door as Joseph kissed Willow and Carla goodbye.

"When should I expect you back?" asked Willow.

"Probably a couple hours," Joseph said.

CHAPTER 9

It was only a few minutes' drive to the house right next to
the chapel. Instead of the standard red brick building, this
one had white stone on the façade in big pieces. I guessed it
had been built in the '50s, before the current architectural
rules for chapels was in place. A part of me liked it purely
because it was different, but another part of me found the
hugeness of the stones a bit too grandiose.

I got out of the car, grabbed hold of Joseph's arm, and held
on tight. I felt shakier than I'd realized I would, perhaps out
of anger.

Joseph rang the doorbell.

A very tall older man, gray around his temples, opened the
door. I noticed as he shook Joseph's hand that he was missing
most of his right middle finger, and in the back of my mind I
wondered briefly how he managed certain temple hand-
shakes that required the use of that finger. Did he do them
with his left or just skip them?

"Brother Wallheim, so good to see you," he said. I realized
I didn't even know Jonathan's last name.

How were we supposed to have this conversation with

Jonathan's father—whom I presumed this was—poking his head in? I started to think of a list of ways to get him out of the house on pretext. Maybe I could ask him to help me with something and leave Joseph with Jonathan.

"And this must be your lovely mother," he said, offering his hand to me.

I shook it, wishing he weren't one of those men who held so tightly. I didn't feel lovely at all and doubted I looked it. I should have been pleased with the chivalry anyway, I suppose.

As it turned out, I didn't have to think of a way to get him to leave.

He said, "Come in. Sit. I'll get out of your way. I just wanted to say hello. Jonathan told me that you and your mother have some questions about Sabrina Jensen you wanted to ask. I think you'd all be more comfortable without me here."

I was surprised that Joseph hadn't made up a more palatable lie. But the man seemed to have no idea of the darkness of what we were going to be asking about or the potential damage to his son's future.

"I'm going to be out front working on our Christmas lights on the roof. We've got a line that's gone dark, and I can't afford to hire Brother Jensen to help us with it."

I tensed at the thought of him working outside on the roof when it was so cold and snow might start falling at any moment. The forecast had said we had a storm coming in soon, hence the wind. And he wasn't a professional like Clint Jensen.

Jonathan came out, nearly an exact replica of his father. Same height, same big shoulders, same wide light-blue eyes.

Had all his fingers in full, though. He waved at his father, then sat on the couch, his body language tight and unyielding.

Joseph spoke very quietly when he opened with, "We're here to talk to you about Sabrina Jensen. She's gone missing."

"Yeah, you said that on the phone," Jonathan said impatiently. "I don't know anything about where she went."

"I understand that you and Peyton were both dating her a few months ago," Joseph said. "Even though she was only fifteen."

"It wasn't really dating. We just went out in groups."

I made an indignant sound at this truth combined with lie, and Jonathan stared hard at me. I couldn't help but think of Satan in the temple film, who never lied directly but always avoided the real truth. Jonathan probably hadn't seen the film at his age but was copying the act so well.

"So there was nothing special about your relationship with Sabrina?" Joseph asked after a moment.

Jonathan shifted uneasily. "We haven't been out with her in months," he said, glancing at the door his father had gone out. "She isn't part of our group anymore. She changed. Started swearing at us and acting—crazy."

I'll bet she had. "So you're saying that you had nothing to do with the change in her behavior?"

Jonathan feigned innocence well. "What could I have done?"

I had little hope that this would work. "You and Peyton were upset that she wouldn't choose between you. So you punished her."

"What did you do to her? Did you exile her from the group?" Joseph asked, scaling back my accusation.

"No, we didn't do anything like that. She's the one who left. She went off with those other two friends of hers. Henry and what's her name—Betty?" He waved a hand.

"Bella," I corrected without thinking.

"Sabrina is missing from home now. She's been gone for nearly a week in this cold weather," Joseph put in. "Something must have happened to trigger that. And I think it has to do with you and Peyton and the rest of the group."

He was skirting around the issue, using weasel words just like Kurt would have. *Something must have happened.* That something had a name.

Jonathan squirmed a bit. "Look, I don't know why she left. Like I said, she hasn't been in our group for months. Now, can I go to back my room and do my homework? If I don't, my grades will fall."

Yes, his grades would fall, poor kid. And then maybe he wouldn't get into the college he wanted to attend after his mission.

"You're a monster," I said, my voice level but my tone vicious. "What you did to her is unforgivable. Don't think there's any number of baptisms you can do that will make you acceptable to the kingdom of God after this."

Jonathan had already started to rise. Then he turned to me. "You're just like she was. Blaming everyone but herself."

He disappeared down the hallway. I thought I'd still be shaking, but I was too angry even for that. I wasn't sure if I believed in the celestial kingdom anymore, but it was one of the church's most sacred beliefs, and he hadn't even batted an eye when I'd threatened him with losing it.

"Let's go," Joseph said.

I wanted to hit something but waited until we got to the car. I started punching the door when we reached it.

Joseph tried to offer a bit of comfort. "We still have Peyton. We might be able to get him to talk. I've always thought he was a follower, not a leader."

CHAPTER 10

Joseph drove to the next house, which was much smaller and older, more of a 1940s bungalow. Outside of the house was a battered-looking pinkish-bronze Toyota that I for some reason assumed was Peyton's. This place seemed so ordinary somehow.

Joseph knocked and the door was opened by a young man. He was clean shaven; had a very short, even missionary haircut; and was tall and lanky in a way that reminded me of Samuel.

That made me think of missions. It was December of this young man's senior year. He might already have turned in his mission papers and been headed out into the field next summer. And if he didn't have a police record, no one would stop him from going.

"Can we sit down with you?" Joseph asked, since Peyton hadn't thought to ask us in.

"What do you want to know?" Peyton asked, sitting gingerly on the couch, his Adam's apple bobbing visibly in his throat.

"It's about Sabrina Jensen," Joseph said.

"You said that on the phone already. I don't know where she is, if that's what you think." He was defensive now, his hands together in his lap.

"It's about why she left," I put in.

"But—" Peyton started, then stopped guiltily, or at least I thought so.

Good, we'd come to the right one.

"I think Sabrina hurt you," Joseph said. "When she refused to choose between you and Jonathan."

Hurt them? Took away some of their feeling of ownership over her, maybe.

"We weren't dating her officially or anything. I mean, she's only fifteen," Peyton blurted out.

Did he really think her being under official dating age was the issue here? I didn't know the legal age of consent in Utah, but none of this mattered when talking about rape.

"I'm sure you thought she was being selfish," Joseph said in a more conciliatory tone.

I twitched at this, but it was obviously the right thing to say. The boy turned to Joseph and seemed to relax.

"Maybe you thought she just needed to learn a lesson," my son added.

I felt sick at how sympathetic he seemed. I couldn't let it go, even for the sake of getting Peyton to confess.

"Rape isn't a lesson," I said quietly.

Peyton jumped a bit, then tried to sit still again. He wasn't entirely successful. His Adam's apple bobbed convulsively as he gave an excuse.

"It wasn't like that," he said. "It was just . . . sex." His face paled, but he looked pleadingly at Joseph. "I know we're not supposed to have sex, but it was just the one time, and it didn't mean anything. It's not something I need to confess or anything. I can still go on my mission." The last two sentences sounded more like questions than statements.

If this were my son, I'd have called a lawyer to protect him, I thought for a moment.

But no. No, I wouldn't have. I would have taught him what was right.

So we went on.

"Did she give consent?" Joseph pressed. "To you or Jonathan or the others?"

Peyton winced. "Well, she'd stopped talking once Jonathan was finished."

"Did she say no?" I asked. "To him."

"Sure, but—" He couldn't get out anymore, it seemed.

"Then it was the opposite of consensual, Peyton. That's not just sex," Joseph said. "It's rape." The words rang heavy.

There was a long moment of silence in which I wished I could break something, preferably one of Peyton's bones.

"I'm sorry," he finally whispered.

"Who were the others? Besides you and Jonathan?" Joseph continued in an even tone. I was angry he was so calm, even though I knew it was necessary to get Peyton to open up more than Jonathan had. I hoped the fury inside him would get him to expose these boys for what they were.

Peyton's leg bounced. "Jonathan invited them all. Just to watch. He thought it would embarrass Sabrina more if other people knew, saw it firsthand. But then . . . it got out of control."

"Did you really think it was right, doing that to her?" Joseph asked.

If Peyton and Jonathan were in his Sunday School class, he'd seen them every week for nearly a year. Of course he'd never guessed they would do something like this, even if there was some hint or rumor of their involvement with Sabrina. No wonder she wouldn't tell him what had happened. She must have thought that Joseph would take their side.

"I know you were baptized and given the gift of the Holy Ghost. That you know right from wrong," Joseph said stalwartly.

A tear streaked down Peyton's face.

"How many of you were there?" Joseph asked.

"Eight," Peyton said in a hollow tone.

I felt the hot tears running down my cheeks now.

"You knew all of them?" Joseph said.

Peyton nodded.

"All right. Now, I can't force you to do anything as your Sunday School teacher, but I feel strongly that you need to confess to Bishop Harmon about this. Let him talk about what you can do to make amends. About your missions."

I tightened my jaw. I thought I'd made it clear I wanted Joseph to convince Peyton and Jonathan to officially confess to the police. But maybe this was the first step. Would the bishop excuse them easily or pressure them to face legal consequences? I didn't know him, but Joseph did, and I decided to trust his judgment.

Peyton put his fingers up to his mouth and started chewing. I saw then that he had already bitten his fingernails to the quick. Was it an old habit or a new one?

I stood up. I couldn't take this anymore. I had to pace, though I tried to do it behind the couch so as to be less distracting.

"God has infinite mercy," Joseph said. "And if you truly want to serve in good faith, you need to be honest about your sins. Otherwise, how can you ever truly overcome them?"

Good. It was too bad Mormons didn't believe in hell, or I'd wish Peyton and the others there. There or to Outer Darkness, where the worst of the betrayers went. But neither of them had a sure enough knowledge of Christ to belong there—a pity. In Outer Darkness, they'd be condemned to an eternity of solitude, away from all family and friends, and cut off from the presence of God, Christ, and the Holy Ghost. The fear of that might do something to these privileged, selfish young men.

"All right," Peyton said. "I'll go talk to the bishop."

"And tell him everything," Joseph said.

Peyton's head bowed.

"But before we go, I want you to give me the list of names," he said. He took a tiny notepad and a pen out of his pocket and handed it to Peyton.

I held very still as I waited to see if Peyton would do what Joseph asked. To my relief, he took the pen and notepad and began to write down the names shakily in two columns.

When he was finished, he handed the list to Joseph. "I think that's all of them." His voice had turned into a whisper. "I didn't mean for it to go that far. I wish I could forget all of it."

He wanted to forget? What about Sabrina?

Joseph stood up and took the list, then patted Peyton gently on the knee. "Thank you. This is the first step of real repentance. It's the only hope you have of coming clean with God. You know that with God, nothing is impossible. Not even forgiveness for this."

Were we already talking about forgiveness? Had I missed something?

Joseph guided me out again, and when we got to the car, he said, "Maybe he'll talk Jonathan into confessing, too. Once Peyton goes to the bishop and confesses."

Or maybe Jonathan would get Peyton to recant. I'd been so glad that we had that list when we'd walked out of Peyton's house, but now I wondered what value it held as evidence.

"It's a start, Mom."

"You think that if those boys all confess and are punished, that Sabrina will want to come back?" I asked, unsure.

"Well, what else can I do?" he asked.

I had no idea what more any of us could do at this point.

CHAPTER 11

Joseph started driving back to his house. I felt defeated and thought again about what I could do for Sabrina to make sure she felt safe somewhere, anywhere in this world.

When we pulled up to Joseph's garage, we saw a nearly new, dark-colored BMW waiting on the street with its lights on.

"Oh God," Joseph said.

Which meant he knew who it was. But I didn't figure it out until he'd stopped his car, pocketed his keys, and said to me, "Mom, you stay here while I handle Jonathan."

How could my own son know me so poorly? Then again, it was exactly the thing Kurt would have said, and he'd known me far longer than Joseph.

I got out of the car to see Jonathan walking toward us, his hands in his pockets, an air of nonchalance that had to have been carefully affected in his gait.

"Peyton called me as soon as you left his house," Jonathan announced. "He told me what he said to you. And about that list of names he gave you."

"You need to repent," Joseph repeated firmly. "Go to the bishop and confess."

I felt like I'd already been on this merry-go-round, so I took advantage of the fact that Jonathan wasn't paying attention to me, turned my back to the two men, and got out my phone. I hit RECORD, put the phone in my coat pocket, and turned back.

"I'm going on a mission, like my father wants. I'm going to college after that, where he'll pay for my degree. And then he's going to give me a job at his company. Because I'm his son, and he trusts me with the family business. Even by the time he dies, he's not going to know about any of this," Jonathan said calmly.

"He's going to find out. Better you tell him now," Joseph said, "and ask for his forgiveness."

"Not going to happen," Jonathan said. It was strange seeing him in the twilight of the porch lights. His facial features seemed sharper, like in a black-and-white Bela Lugosi horror movie.

"You can't ignore this. The police are going to look into this list as soon as Sabrina comes forward."

Jonathan let out a bark at this, almost a laugh. "She isn't going to tell the police anything. We talked it over."

So that was what the threats had been about—the group had been trying to scare Sabrina into keeping quiet.

Joseph's whole body was tense. "She's only fifteen, Jonathan. You're eighteen. How could you do that to her?" he asked.

"She was a bitch," Jonathan said simply.

The words hung in the air like icicles, no chance of them ever melting.

"Because she wouldn't pick one of you," Joseph said.

Because she wouldn't do what they wanted. Because she believed that she belonged to herself. The crime of practically every woman in the history of the world, I thought bitterly.

"She got what she deserved," Jonathan said. "And you should stay out of this if you know what's good for you." He waved a hand at Joseph's house.

Was that a threat? I was doubly glad I had turned on my phone to record.

"You think she deserved to be treated like she didn't matter? Like she was garbage?" Joseph asked.

"She was garbage. *Is* garbage," Jonathan said.

This wasn't enough. Nothing that Jonathan had said yet was proof. I had to make sure he admitted it outright. So I stepped in, angling my coat pocket as close to Jonathan as I could without it being obvious.

"You raped her. You got your friends together to make sure they helped you with that lesson for her, isn't that right?" I asked.

"So what if I did?" he asked.

He planned it, I thought. Even if Peyton hadn't realized it, Jonathan had cold-bloodedly planned the entire thing.

"She never said yes, did she?"

"No," he said, almost laughing. "She screamed for me. She didn't scream for the others. But I knew she liked it. That's what girls like her always want. She wouldn't choose between us because she wanted us both. Well, she got all of us."

She screamed because she wanted it. *Because that was what girls like her always wanted.* There was nothing she could have said that would have made him imagine she didn't want him.

I hoped my phone hadn't stopped recording or run out of battery. Was that enough?

"You didn't even think to use condoms," I said. "What if she's pregnant? What if she gets a paternity test? Then your confession won't matter. The proof will be there," I said coldly.

Jonathan twitched at that. "She said she wanted it. She was begging for it." He was changing his story. I had already gotten as much as I was going to.

I sighed. My heart felt like it had burned up in my chest, becoming a lump of black coal.

"I really did believe that there was still some spark of goodness in you," Joseph said. Then he turned his back on Jonathan, and we walked inside. I pulled out my phone and stopped recording, my back turned to Joseph. I wasn't sure I was ready to let him know what I'd been doing.

"You're not worried about him doing anything to Willow or Carla, are you?" I asked, turning back to him.

"No," Joseph said, more hopeful than certain. "He wouldn't do that. He's not stupid."

Wasn't he?

"But what happened here," Joseph went on, "reflects on the safety of the entire ward. How can I feel safe sending my own daughter to church activities one day with when the young men at them could do something like this to her? There's no safety for young women out there. None."

I couldn't deny this truth, even if I'd tried for a long time.

He thought for a moment, then added, "I'm going to go to the temple tomorrow. I'll take off another day from work. I have to make this right and ask God for the right words to say to these young men. They must never forget what they did."

"And then you're taking the list to the police, right?" I said. I had the recording, and I would bring that in as evidence, too, when the time was right. After Joseph had gone in with the list and made sure they would listen. If not, my approach would be a second shot.

"Do you really think Sabrina wants to have a long, drawn-out court case—or worse, eight of them—where she has to relive this again and again?" Joseph asked in return.

"You think she isn't doing that already?" I asked. "Every minute of her life without any justice."

"It's not the same," Joseph said.

He was right about that. It *wasn't* the same.

"She needs to believe in people again. She needs to be able to trust the system," I said. That was the only thing I could imagine that would help get her back into a home, even if not her parents'.

Joseph nodded. "All right. I'll call the police. I'll give them the list. And Henry's and Bella's information. I don't know how far they'll get without Sabrina, but we can get them started. And maybe they'll be able to find her."

This was a big step for Joseph, and he would face serious consequences in his ward. The names on that list alone could make him a vector for hate. But then again, he was an adult, a man with a certain amount of power of his own. He had a lot more to risk but a lot less to lose than Sabrina already had.

"I think I'll just head home," I said.

"There's one thing I didn't tell you," Joseph said, his hand on the door.

"What's that?"

"The names on the list. One of them is the bishop's son. And another is the son of the stake president."

I stopped in my tracks. No wonder Joseph was worried

about consequences. "How do you think the fathers will react?" I asked, reaching out a hand for his arm. "Will they listen to the truth?"

He shook his head. "I don't know. The bishop—he's a good man, and I think he knows his son has done some bad things already. But the stake president—his son is the student body president at school, for heaven's sake. He's gotten early acceptance to Harvard, which he's going to defer for a mission. He's the golden boy of the whole stake. Parents are practically lining up for their daughters to date him."

Of course they were. But maybe they would all learn something from this. That credentials didn't make you good or worthy. And young women could have their own good sense about which young men to go out with. Parents would do better to listen to that, I thought.

"You're doing the right thing, Joseph," I said.

"Yeah." He let out a long breath. "I hope so. This could destroy the whole stake."

I was tired of that excuse. Letting victims be ignored because it saved the church. Specifically the men of the church. Not anymore. Not when I had a hand in speaking out. "If the truth destroys something, then it probably wasn't real to begin with," I said. Didn't one of our own church leaders say that? Or something like it?

Joseph recoiled. "Mom, how can you say that? The church does lots of good around here. But if people start throwing accusations and stop trusting each other, it might be years before we can help each other again. And that's not even considering the issue of the media getting involved. This could make national headlines."

Kurt would say the same thing. But Kurt wasn't the one Joseph had called. That had been me. And I wasn't interested in protecting the Mormon Church anymore. Too many cases like this that had been swept under the rug, year after year, generation after generation. Women of all ages had been told for long enough that their pain didn't matter. It pushed me even further from my faith. Surely Christ hadn't died on the cross just so we could keep having nice Christmas potlucks and choir rehearsals.

But my son was the one making the sacrifices here to help Sabrina. I understood that. He had more to lose than I did. "I have never been prouder of you, Joseph. You've grown up to be exactly the kind of man I hoped." I kissed his cheek. I knew it wasn't much, but it was true.

"I'll keep you in the loop," Joseph said, looking shaken but determined. "You know, if we three have to move in with you and Dad because the house gets burned down." He said it jokingly, but I wasn't so sure.

"You're welcome anytime. You know we have the space," I said. I waved at him as I walked back to my own car, then drove home. The Christmas lights all up and down the valley just didn't seem to sparkle like they had before, and when I passed the temple, I wondered exactly what God thought of our Christmas celebrations.

CHAPTER 12

I slept fitfully and woke up very late. Kurt had already left for work, and I hadn't mentioned anything about Sabrina Jensen. I could have sent him the basics in a text, but I knew this was more of a face-to-face conversation. Joseph texted me shortly afterward to tell me he was at the Ogden police station and that he'd call and tell me all about it when he was finished.

I did some laundry and cleaning, then decided it was time to go back to the Main Library in downtown Salt Lake City where Henry and Bella had met Sabrina. I couldn't just wait around for the police to start their search.

God had put me in this position, and even if I had problems believing in the church, I didn't have a problem believing in God. Helping strangers in dangerous situations had become my calling. Even Joseph had known that when he phoned me instead of his own ward members. God had whispered to him because God hadn't forgotten Sabrina. He'd sent me.

And if I couldn't convince her to come home, maybe I could talk her into staying with us until things were resolved on the legal front. I texted Kurt and lied outright, saying I was going to babysit for Joseph and Willow and would stay there for the night.

He only texted back a thumbs-up emoji, which probably meant he was busy with year-end tax stuff. I started gathering supplies for the night, rummaging through the kitchen trying to find useful items. I came across Samuel's old backpack from high school and filled it with crackers and fruit and a couple of water bottles. I threw in a couple of the aluminum foil camp blankets that Kurt and the boys took with them, though I wasn't sure that would really help anyone. I also threw in a wool blanket.

I put on a pair of Kurt's thermal garments, a different style of the traditional Mormon sacred underwear. They were far too long on me, so I had to roll them up at the ankles and wrists.

I felt slightly guilty about this, since I wasn't sure what the rules were about wearing men's garments as a woman. Not to mention the fact that I hadn't worn my own garments in months, but we didn't have any other thermals in the house. Finally, I put sweatpants over my jeans and my warmest coat on top, along with two pairs of gloves and two wool hats.

I was far too warm inside, so I took off the extra layers and put them in the car for when I arrived at my destination.

What about my purse? It seemed foolish to bring it, so I took out my driver's license to put in my back pocket. Then I took out all the cash I had on hand, which was about a hundred and twenty dollars, and poked it into my bra. I really debated about my phone, worried it would be stolen, damaged by the cold, or broken somehow.

In the end, I took it just in case of an emergency. Truth be told, I felt naked and vulnerable without a phone nowadays, even if I had lived most of my life without one.

I took the key off my keyring and tucked it into my back pocket, then got into the car. I looked at our neighborhood differently as I pulled away. I'd always known we lived in a nice area, but it seemed ridiculously luxurious to me now. The snow had been neatly carved from driveways and streets by snowblowers. The houses themselves seemed oversized and nearly brand new. There was steam being released from the chimney of every home, rising out into the cold.

I could also see blinking red lights on many of the homes, indicating security systems. There were motion-sensor lights on most garages. Wrought-iron or picket fences added an extra layer of protection from break-ins. And why? So we could protect what we owned from everyone else.

And what about all the scriptures that talked about not depending on worldly wealth but trusting in God to provide the barest necessities? We certainly didn't seem to be practicing that. Sometimes, it seemed like the best parts of the Mormonism from my childhood were no longer practiced. On the other hand, though there had certainly been terrible parts of Mormonism that had been changed, too. At least African Americans could go to the temple now.

I passed by my former friend Anna Torstensen's house and up the hill we used to climb together twice a week, driving slowly in case there was ice on the road. Then I went down the mountain, got onto the freeway, and headed north toward downtown Salt Lake City. I was sweating from all my layers as I pulled into the library parking lot, but by the time I stepped out of the car, I was shivering—and I knew it would only get worse. It was already fifteen degrees Fahrenheit and was supposed to go below zero later tonight.

I locked the car, closed the doors. Then I put on my coat and the two pairs of gloves and hats and caught a glimpse of myself in one of the mirrors as I headed up to the mall level. I could barely see my face under all this clothing. I might actually be able to get by without sticking out.

The Salt Lake City Main Library took up most of a city block. It was an incredibly beautiful piece of modern architecture, all glass and soaring white stone. It looked like a majestic bird, reaching for the clouds, with wings draped along the grass and earth below its feet. On the east side, there were bike racks and a fountain—and several windbreaks that were perfect for the homeless. Right now, I could see shopping carts filled with sleeping bags and clothes, their owners asleep or slumped in easy chairs in the stacks inside.

I walked around the eastern side of the building along the grass and then headed to the upper level, where I could see many people huddled near carts in a row along the overlook to the fountains and the library's main level.

"Can I help you?" asked one of the young men, curly hair coming out of the knit hat on his head. He waved a hand at me, and I noticed he was dressed in multiple layers, like me. But if I'd thought that I would pass as someone coming to squat here, he seemed to see through that immediately. I wanted to ask about Sabrina right away, but he wasn't much older than she was, and it seemed callous.

"Are you all right?" I asked.

"It's not bad today," he said flatly.

I wondered what he meant. "How so?"

He shrugged. "The police haven't bothered us as much as usual—it's probably too cold out. Usually, they come through every few hours to make sure we're not sleeping outside. It's against the law, so if we're under a blanket, they can run us off."

"It's illegal to sleep outside?" I asked. So if you accidentally fell asleep outside, the police could jail you for it? But, of course, it wouldn't be enforced across the board—just a law that enabled the police to force the homeless off public property.

"It is. I know the local Salt Lake City laws. I've read up on all of them. The police are pretty surprised when I quote statutes back to them. They think we don't know. And sometimes *they* don't even know what the laws are. It kind of scares them." He smiled faintly at me.

"I'm sorry," I muttered.

"Not your fault," he said. "I got here at five this morning." He pointed to a sign. "It says right there that the park is open at five A.M., but the police came by at five-ten and told us all we had to leave. Like they thought we couldn't read? I pointed out the sign, and they got mad and told us we didn't belong here. But they couldn't drag us out."

"Good move," I said. He seemed so smart, and I caught myself wondering why he was homeless before realizing my own prejudices about who ended up on the street. There were so many cases that had to do with luck and circumstances outside anyone's control.

He shrugged. "I try to help out the others. They don't know how to protect themselves."

"Where do you sleep if you're not allowed to sleep outside?" I asked, delaying bringing up Sabrina's name.

"Don't sleep much," he said. I looked a little closer and realized his eyes were sallow.

"Do you have enough food? Do you go to the any of the kitchens?" I'd volunteered to serve lunch at a homeless kitchen once. I'd thought of myself as so kind. It now seemed selfish and blind somehow.

"Sometimes," he said. "But you're always hungry when you're up all night, walking around in the cold. There's never enough food, but we try to store some in our carts to keep us going."

I thought of the backpack and felt guilty that I wasn't sharing.

"Is there anything I can do to help?" I thought of the cash in my bra. I wanted to give him some but was afraid to flash money here. What if someone took it or even hurt me to get it?

But that was an unfair assumption.

"Oh, I don't need much. Mostly I just want to have a cup of hot chocolate on a night like this. They'll kick us out in a couple of hours, and then we'll have to roam around trying to find a spot where we're safe."

I turned to the side, hoping to hide my hand reaching into my bra. I got out a five-dollar bill, hesitated, and then got out another ten. I tucked the rest back into my bra and turned back to face him. He was looking discreetly away from me, and I wished he hadn't noticed what I was doing, but I clearly hadn't been subtle enough.

"Let me give you this," I said, holding out the bills.

He quickly accepted the money. "Oh, thank you so much. I really didn't expect anything," he said, which immediately made me think that he had.

But so what if he had?

"I'd give you a hug if it weren't for the fact that I didn't think you'd enjoy it much, considering the smell."

"I would like a hug, actually," I said. Was that creepy of me, wanting a hug from a stranger the same age as Samuel, whom I missed so desperately?

He hugged me firmly, and I got a faint smell of something I hadn't recognized before. Something sweet and smoky. Marijuana? Something I wasn't well acquainted with.

"Thanks again. So much," he said, pocketing the money.

"Sure," I said and then hesitated. "Hey, I'm looking for someone. A young girl named Sabrina. She used to live in Ogden, but I thought she might be around here. You wouldn't happen to know her, would you?"

"Sabrina?" he said as if it sounded familiar.

I got out my phone despite stiff cold fingers and showed him the only photo I had of her.

He squinted and tipped the phone this way and that. "I don't know. Maybe," he said.

"Two of her friends said she came to the library during the day sometimes. To charge her phone and take a nap."

His head lifted. "Oh, yeah. The ones with phones do that," he said, sounding a little envious.

"Did you see her here today at all?"

He shook his head. "Sorry," he said.

"But if she's around here once in a while, do you have any idea where else she might hang out?" I was desperate for another clue. I couldn't keep wandering aimlessly downtown.

"There are some kids who hang out around the Gateway," he said. "And at Pioneer Park."

I waited a moment, hoping for more, but there was nothing. "Thank you," I said.

"Sure," he said and turned away.

It was now well past dark. I headed west toward Gateway Mall as he'd suggested. I passed a set of elders on State Street, waiting for the local light-rail, TRAX. They were a common enough sight in Utah: dark suits, white shirts, and name tags. The crewcut hair and smiling faces. They had gloves on but no hats, and I couldn't help but think of my Samuel in the cold Massachusetts winter. Was he out tonight?

I turned back and hurried toward them. I had a rush of anxiety as I did it, the thought that I might be missing Sabrina by not continuing forward. But I couldn't do that without stopping to talk to the elders.

"It's cold out. Are you two going to be all right?" I asked. It was virtually the same question I'd asked the young man whose name I'd never gotten at the Main Library, but it felt completely different.

"Oh, we're fine, thanks," said the taller one.

"You're sure? You don't need something to eat?" I thought about the food I had in my backpack. With a pang of guilt, I wondered why I felt so much more comfortable sharing it with these elders than the young man at the library who'd mentioned hot chocolate.

"We're fine. Are you a missionary mom?" the tall one asked.

He had me pegged, even in my disguise of sorts. "Yes," I said.

"We would have asked you if you wanted to hear about the Book of Mormon, but it seemed pretty obvious you already had," said the Polynesian elder with no discernable accent.

"I'm a member. My name is Linda Wallheim," I said and held out a hand.

They shook it in turn. "Sister Wallheim, where is your son serving? Or is it your daughter?"

"My son," I said, struggling not to flinch at the word *daughter*, thinking of Georgia, long gone. "Samuel. He's in Boston."

"Oh," they nodded. "That's a hard one."

"You think Utah's not hard?" I asked.

They smiled at each other as if at a secret. Then the tall one said, "Not really. Everyone already knows Mormons around here. We don't have to work as hard to convince them we're actually Christian. And most of the people here don't hate Mormons or think we're cultish because they see us every day."

"Well, that's good."

He put up a hand. "And before you ask, yes, we actually do have a lot of baptisms. But we don't do much tracting anymore because we have so many referrals from members. Which is why missionaries in other areas say it's not fair, that it's too easy for us. We have no idea what it's like to get a door slammed in our face or have people set their dogs on us. And I'm kinda okay with that. How about you, Elder Tonga?"

Elder Tonga said he also liked Utah and serving a mission and that he was very grateful to for being able to serve God in this way. Most of the time, missionaries were sent away from home to focus on their missions, and those from outside the United States were usually sent here to learn more about the heart of the Mormon world.

The TRAX train pulled up then, and the elders got inside,

waving goodbye to me. The train seemed to leave warm air behind—even if it was stale—and I felt a little extra push of energy.

The Gateway was packed with shoppers, but I could see pockets of people in dirty clothes, asking for money or huddled against buildings, wrapped in blankets and trying to stay warm. I didn't go around asking for Sabrina this time. Instead, I walked around carefully, turning around occasionally as if I'd gotten lost or confused when what I was actually doing was scanning faces.

I also saw a few teenage boys who looked like they were about to pull out skateboards and coast through the center mall area. They had on hoodies, not regular coats, and their pants were hanging down past their butts, which I had to think was cold.

It was nearly ten by the time I moved on from the Gateway, determining that if Sabrina was there, I couldn't find her. I felt a rumbling in my stomach, a reminder I hadn't had dinner.

So I got out the backpack and took out a couple of granola bars, wrestling with the packages through double gloves, which was no fun, but determined not to let my bare hands touch the freezing air. Ultimately, my teeth were very useful, though I felt a little bad about letting a few little wrapper pieces fly away as litter. I managed to get one of the bottles of water open and drank quickly before putting it away.

It was nowhere near as satisfying as a home-cooked meal. My stomach felt hollow, even though I could practically feel the sugar sitting in there. I wished there had been less of that and more . . . well, food.

I walked down 400 West. There were fewer shoppers out

this late but still plenty of cars, presumably coming home from various holiday concerts, parties, photo ops with the lights, and church groups meeting on Temple Square.

All my body wanted was for me to go home and go to sleep. To be horizontal, not vertical. What my soul wanted was not to be afraid. It wanted to find Sabrina and make sure she was safe.

Keep moving. Keep moving, I told myself. Where else had he said to try? Oh, yes. Pioneer Park. That was south of the Gateway.

As I turned onto the open street, I saw a group of young women, or perhaps not so young—I couldn't tell. They were wearing far too little for a night like tonight, though at least they had leggings on and long sleeves with furry gloves. No fashionable holes in their clothing, but no scarves or hats, either. I didn't cross to the other side of the street, but I didn't slow down as I passed by them. I found myself holding my breath, although they didn't smell of anything but too much perfume, an assault I dealt with regularly at church.

A car stopped just as I passed, and once its window was rolled down, one of the young women called out, "Eighty bucks."

"Sixty," said the man in the car.

"Bastard," said the young woman. But she got into the car anyway, its engine loud and ragged as it passed me.

Of course, Sabrina Jensen could already have gone off with a man like that. I shuddered to think about this in the wake of what had happened. The repercussions could be as bad or even worse than the triggering event.

She was so young. At fifteen, I'd never even kissed a boy.

I'd never gone on a date, and I'd had only the vaguest idea what sex was.

A few years ago, there had been a new category added to the Young Women's program: Virtue. I hated it. We didn't need to add more pressure to Mormon purity culture. I didn't particularly approve of casual sexual encounters for teens, but I also thought that consent and protection were more important to learn than guilt and shame.

A gust of wind hit me as I crossed the street in front of Pioneer Park, and I felt sure for a moment I was going to end up facedown in the middle of the street while cars honked and—if I was lucky—drove around me. Somehow, I stayed on my feet, gasping through clenched teeth, and made it to the other side.

"Nice coat, Mother," said a white-haired man with several layers on. He nodded to me as I stared into the vast darkness of the park. Around its edges were businesses, but the park itself was only grass and trees—and green Porta Potties, which the city had put there out of necessity. There were a lot of figures chatting near the trees, huddling together for warmth. No one was moving much, but not many looked asleep, either. I saw a mass on the ground wrapped in a blanket and worried I had found a dead body, but after a few minutes, it moved slightly, and I sighed relief.

Farther in toward the center of the park, away from the eyes of the casual drivers-by (or the police), I could see some tents set up and wondered how much real protection they offered at this time of year. In the dim moonlight, I could see people shooting up with needles right out in the open. I could also see some fires set up in the big metal garbage cans.

As I got closer, I could see the people surrounding the fires, slowly turning to get all of their bodies warmed. I was tempted to slide in myself. My toes were so cold inside my boots that they felt like pieces of ice I was dragging around. My hands weren't as numb because I'd been trying to increase circulation to them with constant fist clenching, but they were still buzzing with pins and needles of cold.

I checked my watch again. Almost 11 P.M. now. The streets were getting a little quieter, but I could hear the whoosh of the interstate just a few blocks away.

The backpack that I'd brought thinking it would be useful sat like a heavy chain around my neck. My back ached, and my shoulders felt like they had blisters ready to burst at the point where the straps pulled. I was too old for this kind of thing.

"You don't belong here," said a very tall, broad man with a kind of haphazard tie around his neck over a sweatshirt. He stood in front of me, blocking my way.

"I'm new," I said, too scared to look him directly in the face. "I've never been here before." I tried to move around him, but he was fast, too.

I looked up at him and saw suspicion in his eyes. "What are you doing here? You a reporter? Doing some kind of story about living with the homeless at the holidays?"

I noticed now that he had fingerless gloves on and that his fingers were long and lean and delicate, like an artist's.

"I'm looking for someone," I admitted, since my first pretense hadn't gone too well.

"Who? One of your kids? He an addict?"

"It's my daughter," I said, and as I said it, it felt like the truth. "She's only fifteen." My voice broke. "I just want to bring her home."

"Fifteen?"

I nodded, putting in all my effort not to cry since the tears would freeze right on my face.

"You could try the gas station over there." He gestured to the Fast Break on 300 West. "There's a group there. Asks for money, goes inside and buys food. The convenience store's open all night, if you have an excuse for being inside."

I felt a sharp moment of hope. Maybe all my wandering around had been leading to this, and now I'd be able to help Sabrina at last.

I turned back to the kind man. "Thank you." I hesitated. "You don't sleep at night, do you?" I asked, remembering what the young man at the library had said.

He let out a breath through his nose, shaking his head. "Not in the winter. If you want to stay alive, you keep moving and sleep during the day. Inside, if you can find a place."

My mind flashed to Sabrina, alone and out in the cold. I turned toward the gas station.

"I'll come with you," said the man. He held out his hand. "Lyle," he said.

"Linda," I told him and shook it.

We walked toward the Fast Break. I was sure I could hear my legs protesting the movement. They had been ready to turn into solid ice.

When we stopped at the corner, I picked through the group one by one, looking for anyone Sabrina's height. They were all in their teens or just a little older.

"I'll wait here. You want me to take your backpack and keep it safe?" Lyle said.

I shook my head. It wasn't suspicion on my part—there

were provisions in there for Sabrina if I found her and couldn't get her to leave.

"Why are you helping me?" I asked Lyle.

"You seem like a nice lady," he said with a shrug. "Why shouldn't I help?"

"I haven't done anything for you," I pointed out.

"Don't have to."

"Thank you," I said. "If there's anything I can do for you—" I wanted to get him some money out of what I had, but with these frozen gloved hands, it could take hours.

"Don't say that, like you think we'll never meet again. Just remember me. Look for me once in a while. And treat me like I'm a real person. Say, 'Hi, Lyle,' even if you're with someone else, all right? Look me in the eyes."

"I will," I said, my voice burning in my throat like fire. It struck me so deep, I might have been swearing an oath of obedience in the temple I once found so much power in.

CHAPTER 13

I took a deep breath, then turned back toward the group of teens.

There was Sabrina.

I could see her now, finally. There was no mistaking her, even with all the layers she had on. Her face wasn't covered, and I was sure she was the one I'd seen earlier at the Gateway, though now I could spot her one crooked tooth toward the side of her mouth.

She was so much smaller than the others, a twig in a forest of thick trees.

"Sabrina," I said, stepping forward.

The others immediately gathered around her in a protective circle, tucking her into the center so I could barely see her face. Her eyes were big, and I could see purple bruising on her face, on the left side of her chin leaking up to one of them. Her lips were too red—was that lipstick, or were they chapped and bleeding?

"Sabrina, I'm Joseph Wallheim's mother. He's worried about you. He asked me to come find you," I said.

"What do you want?" said one of the young women in front. She had her hair shaved on one side, and the other side had once been dyed blue. She had five or six piercings on her ears, but only one set was currently filled, with big heavy gold circles that could have been Christmas ornaments. I guessed she was around seventeen.

"I want to talk to Sabrina," I said.

"Sabrina?" the shaved-headed young woman asked.

"It's fine. I'll talk to her," Sabrina said, as if trying to prove her bravery.

"You don't have to. She doesn't own you."

"It's not like that," Sabrina said. I could see the faint stain of a blush on her cheeks, and it took a moment before an answering flush spread across my own face.

But they peeled back, letting her step forward.

A car honked at us, and I remembered that we were in the middle of the parking lot. Looking down, I could see the ground was covered in discarded packaging from convenience-store food bought inside. No one cared about keeping it clean. It must have driven the store owner crazy.

The teens behind Sabrina moved toward the car and held out their middle fingers, then hit its hood and shouted at the driver. The car backed up and revved out to the street.

That wasn't great for business, either.

"Look, I meant what I said. I came to see if you were all right. Joseph and Willow are worried about you." I didn't mention her parents.

Sabrina kept opening her mouth, but she couldn't seem to get any words out. "How's Carla?" she finally said.

"Carla is fine," I said, relieved she seemed okay, though her face looked like skin stretched over bone. "I'm sure she'd like to see you again soon."

Maybe I'd pushed too hard because Sabrina turned away. She was so thin, even with all that clothing on. Her hands, even in gloves, were tiny, and they flitted around like little birds. How could her mother have thought she was gaining weight?

"If you don't want to go home, you can come stay with me for a while. So you can see Carla and Joseph and Willow." I didn't mention anything about Peyton or Jonathan or the police.

"What about my parents?" Sabrina said.

"I won't tell them where you are if you don't want me to." I felt horrible making this promise, but I would have said just about anything to get her to leave with me right then. Safe. That was what mattered, wasn't it?

"I live in Draper. It's about thirty minutes away from here." I gestured vaguely south.

"I know where Draper is. I took Utah Geography," she muttered.

She was talking more now, which seemed promising, so I went on. "My children are all grown up, like Joseph. My youngest son, Samuel, is on a mission in Boston."

If she remembered Willow talking to her about Samuel, she didn't show it.

"So we have a big house there, and it's just me and my husband left in it." I laughed. I decided not to mention he was the bishop of our ward.

She was staring intently at me, taking in every detail of my clothing.

I took off the backpack, which left my muscles protesting

in a wave of cramps. "Here. Take this. There's some food and water."

Her hands trembled, and she grabbed it so suddenly I let out a squeak of surprise. She had one of the granola bars out before I had a chance to say another word and seemed to eat it almost without taking it out of the wrapper, though the wrapper was in her hand afterward. She looked sick for a moment and put a hand to her stomach, then let out a long, low burp.

Sabrina looked back at the others in the group, who were watching intently. The shaved-headed young woman was staring at the backpack.

"That's only for you," I said.

"That's not the way it works," Sabrina said.

"All right, then. If you come back with me, you can leave that with them." It was a false choice I'd just made up, but I hoped she wouldn't notice.

"Go back where?" Sabrina said, sounding a little dazed now.

"To my house. In Draper," I repeated.

"I know that," she said, annoyed. "But how do we get there?"

"My car's in the library parking lot."

Sabrina wrapped her arms around herself. "That's a mile away," she said.

"It's just a few blocks." I could get it and come back here to pick her up, but I suspected she wouldn't be here when I got back. I had to get her to leave with me now, to separate her from the rest of the group, or I'd probably never find her again. Could I call an Uber at this hour? I didn't think TRAX was still running.

"Look, thanks, I really appreciate it. But I can't." She glanced back at the group, and I saw the shaved-headed young woman in front—the apparent ringleader—make a gesture that seemed to indicate they were leaving.

Sabrina paused. I'd thought she was afraid of going home, but it seemed like she was more worried about leaving her friends.

"Why not?" I asked.

"I just can't," she said. "You wouldn't understand."

"S!" yelled the shaved-headed young woman as the group walked off.

Sabrina jumped a couple of inches. "I have to go," she said. "Thanks. Say hi to Carla for me, all right?"

"No!" She was already moving back to the group. I followed, and by the time I got there, the backpack had already been taken from her, its contents in the process of being divvied up.

I reached for Sabrina's arm and missed. I nearly fell down but caught myself and stood up. I told her, "I'm not leaving without you. I'll stay in this parking lot all day and all night until you come with me."

It was one of the stupidest declarations I'd ever made, even worse than when I had told the boys that if they didn't finish their dinners, they'd never be allowed to leave the table again. That one had come back to bite me, too, when I discovered they were all more stubborn than I was.

"You think you can last even one night out here?" asked the shaved-headed young woman with a derisive laugh.

The money, I thought. It could go to good use. I took off my gloves and got out the cash.

"Sabrina, I know you're worried about your friends. Here," I turned to the blue-haired girl, handing her the ninety dollars I had left.

The money disappeared, and all eyes were on Sabrina.

"Sabrina, you should go," said the girl.

"No, Missy. I belong here with you," Sabrina said, head low.

So she had a name, though it seemed oddly feminine and young.

"Sorry, Linda," Sabrina said as she and the group walked off.

I tried to follow but tripped and landed hard on the cement. By the time I'd picked myself up, the group of sad and scary teens was back at the other corner of the block, a few staring at me with threats in their eyes.

I'd found Sabrina, but I couldn't bring her home.

CHAPTER 14

I backed away from the parking lot and found myself back on the other side of the street, where Lyle was still stationed. I rubbed at my face, lucky I hadn't broken any skin—or bones.

"That didn't go so well, did it?" Lyle said.

"Well, you warned me." I could admit defeat now. Sabrina hadn't even looked back to see if I was all right. And why would she? I wasn't anyone to her.

"You leaving now?" Lyle asked.

"I should," I said. It was past midnight, and Kurt was probably worried that I hadn't texted at all. "But I don't want to." I guess I was just too stubborn to do what made sense.

"Well, if you're going to make it through the night, you need to have some protection from the cold," Lyle said. He held out his hand as he led me back across the street. I was reluctant to get too far from Sabrina—there was a chance she'd try to come back and find me if the others weren't watching her. But I also had to be practical.

Lyle helped me to find a place to sit next to the base of a tree with a trash bag he lent me from his own stash to keep the cold from seeping in. "You can't sleep much like that, but you'll be able to rest your legs a bit. And you can watch her from here." He pointed in the direction of the Fast Break.

I did, indeed, have a straight visual shot of the teens in the parking lot. I couldn't see much detail, but I could see new cars driving off, I imagined under the same circumstances I'd just seen.

"I can tell you about Missy," Lyle said.

"That would be helpful," I said, bowing my head and beginning to feel my face go so cold I wasn't sure my lips or tongue would continue to form words clearly for much longer.

"She came here from California," Lyle continued. "Two years ago, in the spring. She said she came because the aid in Utah was better and the people were nicer."

"What kind of aid does she get?" I asked. It couldn't be much because she and the rest of the group were on the street at night in the middle of winter, trying not to freeze.

"Medical services. Food," Lyle said, gesturing to the clinic across the way.

"Ah." I thought for a minute, trying not to shiver. "How old is she, do you think?"

"I think she's still a teen. Probably can't get into adult housing, so she's stuck out here."

And she'd formed a group of teens who protected each other. I couldn't blame her for that. It was probably a good thing that Sabrina had found her when she had.

"How do the police treat them?" I asked.

"Same as most of us. Run us off when they can; threaten to arrest us if necessary."

"Has she ever been arrested?"

Lyle hmmed. "Probably."

Should I get Sabrina's parents or the authorities involved? I worried she would just leave again if I couldn't assure her she would be safe. After all, she'd left once.

"I've seen groups like that before. They just have a lot of growing up left to do," he went on.

"What usually happens?" I wondered how long he had been here to see so many groups pass through.

"A lot of them get into drugs. Dealing at first, for money. And then they get addicted. But that's not the worst possibility."

I waited for him to explain.

"Prostitution and trafficking for girls their age—and boys—is the real danger. That's what I worry about most, that they'll get in the wrong car one day and no one will ever see them again."

I remembered the young women from earlier. An unwanted picture of Sabrina among them popped up in my head. I had to get her out of here. And somehow right the many wrongs she'd been subjected to and prove to her that not all Mormons would turn a blind eye to the gang rape of a fifteen-year-old girl.

But how?

I sat on the ground, feeling the cold seep into my backside and up my spine into my bones for the next several hours. I refused to call Kurt for help. I could do this myself. I watched Sabrina and the other teens ask for money from people who stopped at the Fast Break convenience store.

At some point, the cold stopped hurting and just became a reality. I stopped blowing on my hands or tucking them under my armpits to try to keep them warm. I sank into an almost zen calm, watching the fires in Pioneer Park burn smaller and smaller.

Throughout the park, there were little camps of people who stayed together. There was little movement between groups, however—you belonged in one specific spot, it seemed.

Cars passed by on the street now and then, but they seemed to be part of another world. There were long periods of silence between them. I dozed off occasionally, head dropping to my shoulder. Then I would start awake, neck sore, and shake myself. Lyle had been right—it wasn't safe to sleep in this kind of cold.

"Coffee?" asked Lyle, offering me a bottle that no longer steamed with the lid off.

I shook my head reflexively, then reconsidered. If there was ever a time I needed coffee, it was now. And why should I follow those rules at this point? I'd never believed God cared about this one. So I reached out my hand and took several swallows. It was warm and sweet and felt like pure strength coursing into my veins.

I gave nicknames to the other members of Sabrina's teen group, all six of them. The big, lanky one was Rex, for Rex Harrison. The guy with the glasses and the head turned down was Harry, for Harry Potter. The girl with the red sneakers was Hot Feet because of the way she kept dancing all over the place to keep moving. And the last guy with the massive muscles that bulged even through layers of clothing was Andre, for Andre the Giant's character in *The Princess Bride*. He seemed like the kind of gentle person whose size intimidated more than it was physically used for anything.

Their "donations" didn't seem to be going particularly well tonight. It was cold and close to Christmas, and whatever spirit of the season there was, it didn't extend to this convenience store parking lot.

At a little after 4 A.M., things started to change in the park. The sky wasn't lighting up with dawn yet, but the fires started to go out, and twenty or more who had been standing around them started to move up the street.

"Where are they going?" I asked Lyle.

"To work," he said.

I let out a harsh laugh, and he stared at me. "Oh. What kind of work?" I asked.

"Newspapers."

"They sell newspapers?" It seemed weirdly incongruous for people living on the street. But now that I thought about it, I'd been into the Salt Lake Temple on a couple of occasions at 5 or 6 A.M. and had seen people bundled up tightly, selling newspapers. Some sold the *Salt Lake Street News*, which focused more on issues related to the homeless, but others sold the *Salt Lake Tribune* and the *Deseret News*, our two rival city papers, which I always read first, though I also subscribed to the *New York Times*. The *Tribune* had even won a Pulitzer recently for reporting on the BYU rape scandal. I wondered if Sabrina's situation would ever come to light in the same way.

Were these people being exploited? Would they ever earn enough to get a start in a more lucrative business? To get an apartment? It seemed unlikely. Only enough for a cup of hot coffee and maybe enough food to get through the day.

It was time to try again. Maybe it was the caffeine, but having spent the whole night here, I knew I had to try to get Sabrina to come back with me again.

I stood up and tried to shake out the aches in my back and limbs, shake some warmth back into my whole body.

"Good luck," Lyle said softly.

"You, too," I said, feeling an unexpected sadness at leaving him. I hoped I did see him around so I could say hi. Strange bedfellows, he and I had been.

My heart was in my leaden feet as I hurried across the street. My pulse pounded in my ears, and time seemed to slow.

"Sabrina, please. Let's go," I said as soon as I was within earshot. I felt both hot and nauseous with adrenaline. If I turned my head at just the right angle, I was sure I could see the temple behind some of the other buildings, glowing with its Christmas lights.

To my surprise, Missy moved out of the way.

"Go on, S," Missy said. "I know you want to."

"Missy, I don't. You promised—"

Missy pushed Sabrina toward me before she could say what the promise was. As Sabrina lay sprawled on the ground, I wondered at Missy's sudden, aggressive reaction, helping her up.

"Sabrina, I'll take you to my house. You'll be safe there," I promised her.

There were tears glistening in Sabrina's eyes. "Is this how it has to be?" she asked Missy.

Missy didn't answer, just turned away.

That was when I took action. I grabbed Sabrina's hand and pulled her with me as I moved north, away from the Fast

Break and toward the library parking garage. To my immense relief, she didn't resist.

I started at the sound of an ambulance crossing but kept us moving. I was so afraid that if I paused or let go for even a moment, Sabrina would pull away and vanish. I didn't know if I was strong enough after a night in the cold to chase after her. And if I did, anyone who saw me would probably think I was attacking her.

Sabrina didn't say a word as we started down the ramp to the library parking garage. "It's all right," I kept saying, as much to myself as to her. "We're going to be all right."

Once we got to the car, I put the heat on high and kept it there. I also insisted that Sabrina buckle herself in.

I stopped at McDonald's and debated for a long moment before ordering hot chocolate for both of us. It was one thing to get coffee for myself and another to do it for a Mormon teen.

When the hot drink came, I was still shaking so badly with cold that the hot chocolate spilled all over and me and the seat. I was sure I would never be warm again.

Trying to steady myself, I handed the second hot chocolate to Sabrina, who was still silent. She didn't drink any of it until we got onto the freeway.

I began to notice how much the two of us smelled. First order of business when we got home: hot showers.

I sipped at the last of the hot chocolate in my cup. Finally, I got up the courage to say, "I know what happened. What Peyton and Jonathan and the others did."

She glanced away from me, and I could see her jaw set hard as she tried not to cry. I regretted the words—who was I to make her talk about this?

"You don't have to say anything about it until you're ready. But I'm here to listen if you want. I promise I won't judge you. None of this is your fault."

No response.

"I'm taking you to my house in Draper. Like I said, we've got an extra room. But if you want to go to your house instead and see your parents, let me know."

She still wouldn't say a word.

Slowly, my body started to feel normal again. I eventually turned down the heat and even took off my gloves and hat. It had been a rough night, but I'd done what I had set out to do. I should've been proud. Okay, I'd lied to Kurt and used my own grandchild as an excuse. But Sabrina was safe.

As the sun rose, I looked around the valley stretching out around me. It seemed like the world was gradually turning to color again in the daylight.

I was dripping sweat by the time I pulled up to my driveway, but I didn't take off my coat.

Sabrina clung to my arm as I pulled her out of the car.

"Here we are," I said, wondering if Kurt would be inside. I checked my watch. It wasn't even 7 A.M.

CHAPTER 15

Kurt was in the kitchen when we stepped inside, holding his cell phone to his ear. He put it down as soon as he saw me.

"Oh, here you are," I said lamely, even though I'd seen his truck in the garage. I hadn't had enough time to make up a script for this. His expression told me he knew about my earlier lie.

"What's going on?" he demanded. "Where have you been all night? I called Joseph, and he said you were never scheduled to babysit Carla last night."

I didn't bother with another lie. Nodding at Sabrina, I said, "I was out finding this young woman. Her name is Sabrina Jensen, and she's from Joseph and Willow's ward. She needs our help."

Sabrina was still pretty shaken up, and she didn't hold out a hand to Kurt. He barely glanced at her, which was disappointing. I'd hoped he would care more about helping someone in need than he did about me lying to him about last night.

"What kind of help?" he asked.

"Sabrina ran away from home last week, and Joseph asked me to help find her. She was on the streets downtown, but I convinced her to come here." I didn't even bother explaining why I hadn't mentioned this before now. Kurt knew we had problems as well as I did.

Kurt looked Sabrina more closely now and seemed to melt at the sight of her state. "Are you hungry?" he asked.

I smiled slightly. That was my husband. Straight to the practicalities.

But Sabrina still said nothing.

Kurt gently put a hand on her shoulder—she flinched but only slightly—and led her to one of the stools at the bar, then pushed a plate of scrambled eggs toward her. "I just cooked these. I bet you'll like them. They have lots of cheese."

That was when I thought to check my phone and saw that Kurt had called me no less than eleven times through the night. The first call had been a little after midnight, so apparently the ruse about babysitting Carla hadn't lasted very long.

Sabrina stared at the eggs, then poked at them with the fork Kurt handed her.

"Do you prefer them sunny side up?" he asked. "I can make some that way if you like."

"They're fine," she said, but she didn't eat them. She just moved the pieces around her plate for a while.

How long since she'd been in a kitchen like this? Only a few days, right? Why did she seem so disoriented?

After a few minutes of silence, Kurt glanced up at me. "I have to get into work early this weekend, and there's church stuff this afternoon," he said. "We'll talk about this tonight, all right?"

"Sure," I said, not looking forward to that at all. "I'm going to get Sabrina settled in Zachary's old room, all right?" I wasn't quite ready to have anyone touch Samuel's room yet. He might come back to live with us for a while after his mission was over.

"Fine," Kurt said. He hesitated a long moment, as if trying to decide whether to come over and kiss me. In the end, he did. It was a brief one, his lips only grazing my cheek, but I would take any sign of him thawing.

Kurt left, and I asked Sabrina again if she would prefer her eggs cooked in a different way.

"Can I just have some cereal?" she asked.

I used to have cereal only for days when I didn't feel like cooking but felt terrible offering that to a guest, especially a girl who had spent so many days out in the winter cold in Utah. But if that was what she wanted . . . I opened the cupboard and showed her what we had. An unopened two-year-old box of Cap'n Crunch for Samuel. Great Grains and Grape-Nuts for me and Kurt. The kids used to call the latter "breakfast nails," and I had to admit they were rather crunchy.

"Cap'n Crunch," Sabrina said softly.

I handed it down to her along with a bowl and spoon.

She poured herself a bowl and started in on it as soon as I added milk. She ate noisily for ten minutes, and I had a couple bites of the eggs she hadn't finished, wanting nothing more than to go right to bed, stench be damned.

"Tired?" I asked her as she handed me the bowl to put in the dishwasher.

She nodded.

"Let me show you upstairs, all right?"

She followed silently, so I kept looking behind me to make sure she was still there.

"It's right in here." I opened the door to Zachary's room. He'd put most of his personal items in storage in the basement, but there was still a Utah Jazz poster on the wall.

"It's a boy's room," Sabrina said, putting a hand to the corner of the poster that was coming up.

"Yes, my son Zachary's," I said. "But he's been out of the house for years now."

She said nothing and didn't move toward the bed.

"The sheets are clean and fresh. Or you can have a bath first, if you'd rather."

I wished I hadn't said that because she seemed suddenly very self-conscious, looking down at her clothes and wrinkling her nose. "Bath," she said.

Then I had to find her a fresh towel and show her where the bathroom was. "I'll find you some old pajamas of mine, and you can wear them until your clothes are washed," I said as I left her alone in the bathroom.

I had a brief worry that she might hurt herself in there but put it away.

I could hear the water running as I tried to make myself keep moving. I went down the hall to the master bedroom.

Rummaging through my own drawers, I came up with nothing I thought would fit her tiny waist, so I finally went and looked through Samuel's old clothes and found some sweatpants with a drawstring waist she could cinch up. I left that and an old, plain-colored light blue T-shirt on the bed.

Back in my own room, I took off my smoke-infused coat and

the extra layers, including Kurt's thermal garments, which he'd probably discovered were missing. Would he harangue me about that, as well? I threw them in a pile on the floor, just like my teenagers used to do, and felt righteously defiant. I'd deal with that later. Everything else could come later.

I took a quick shower, just enough to rinse off the smell, then hopped out, nervous that Sabrina might leave at any moment. But no, the other shower was still going. So I sat down on my bed to wait until the water went off but ended up falling asleep like that, slumped over on the side of the bed. I woke up sometime after noon, still groggy. After some negotiation with my brain, I managed to pick up Sabrina's laundry from the bathroom to put in the washing machine, then poked my head into Zachary's room. She was there, asleep—safe. At that, I went back to bed.

About 4 P.M., I woke again, went downstairs, moved her clothes to the dryer, and realized I was starving. I needed to make dinner, but I was too hungry to start. So I got out a Tupperware container of cookie dough from the freezer and feasted on it until I had a sugar headache.

A few minutes later, Sabrina came slowly down the stairs. She looked into the kitchen cautiously. "Hello?" she said. "Mrs. Wallheim?"

"Come on in. And you can call me Linda."

She looked longingly at the frozen cookie dough container.

"It's chocolate chip," I said, "and you're welcome to it." I handed it over.

"Are you sure?" she asked.

"Of course. I'm always making cookies around the holiday season. Never a shortage of that around here."

She used a spoon to scoop out the dough, even though I'd been using my fingers.

"Do you like cooking?" I asked, trying to get an easy conversation going. At some point, I wanted to talk to her about her parents, Jonathan and Peyton, the police. But not now.

"Yes," she said. "At least, when I know the recipe."

"Do you want to help me with dinner?"

"If you want me to," she said tentatively.

"What do you feel like eating? Italian? American? Mexican?" I was fairly confident of my skills in those arenas, though my family was actually Swedish and English.

"Oh, any of those sound good," she said. Her expression was more relaxed now.

"Burritos?" There would be a lot of chopping vegetables for that, which she could do.

She shrug-nodded, and I set to work, taking lettuce, tomatoes, and onions out of the fridge and setting out a cutting board and knife. Before she got started, I sent her down to the storage room for a can of olives. I wanted her to feel comfortable in this house, that there wasn't anything here she couldn't take or any room she wasn't allowed to go into.

She was reluctant to go downstairs, but I called out directions the whole way, and she managed to find the olives. I opened them with a can opener and told her what to do.

Then I started the beans in the pressure cooker because I hadn't set them to soak ahead of time. In an hour, the kitchen smelled wonderful. But I only had to close my eyes to be back at Pioneer Park, with the smells of coffee, drugs, smoke, urine.

I shook myself, then caught Sabrina looking frozen, the knife in her hand but nothing being chopped.

"You okay?" I asked.

She didn't seem to hear me.

Did I dare touch her?

Before I made a choice, there was a loud knock on the front door.

Sabrina started and dropped the knife.

"Mom? Dad said you were here! It's me!"

Sabrina's eyes were huge.

"It's Joseph. Don't be nervous," I said as we listened to Joseph's large shoes clumping toward us. Why was her reaction so fearful? Joseph was a friend, wasn't he? Was she worried he'd try to force her to go back and live with her parents?

"Mom?" Joseph called again.

"In here!" I called out, but by then he was already in the kitchen.

"Sabrina!" he exclaimed, then rushed forward, hands outstretched, to give her a big bear hug.

He noticed after a moment how panicked she was and let his arms fall and pulled back, giving her some space. "I'm so glad you're safe," he said. "You have no idea how worried we were about you. Not just me and Willow. Everyone in the ward. The bishop, Sister Stevenson in the Young Women, your parents, your friends."

How could he be so oblivious as to bring up the whole ward? That included the young men who had driven her out in the first place.

"I didn't want to call your parents until I had seen you," he said. "But now that you're in front of me, I have to let them know you're all right. And the others." He reached for his phone.

"Please, no," she said, her lips hardly moving, her arms wrapped tightly around her stomach.

"Joseph, stop," I said with a steely undertone.

"What? Why?" Joseph asked.

"Please don't tell my parents you found me," Sabrina got out.

Joseph's hand dropped, still holding the phone. "Why not? They're so worried about you. When my dad called me this morning and said my mother had brought you here to sleep, I figured it was just a place for you to rest and clean up before you went home."

"I don't want them to know where I am," Sabrina said, still stiff.

"Okay," Joseph said slowly. "Is there a reason?"

"Yes," she said.

Joseph and I waited.

She flapped hands around. "You can't understand. Either of you. You're both—you have—" she stopped.

"What?" I asked quietly.

She took a deep breath. "Not everyone is like you," she said finally. She looked at Joseph with a pained expression. "I see how you look at Carla. You love her so much. And Willow, too. You're all so, so . . . together."

"Your parents love you, too," Joseph tried to argue.

But Sabrina just shook her head. "They say that, but they don't. I don't even think they love each other. They got married—because they were getting older and they felt like it was the right thing to do. And having a baby was the right thing, too. But once they had me . . ." she trailed off.

"You don't have to go back if you don't want to," I said. I still didn't know what had gone wrong at home with her parents. I'd only noticed the hints of something wrong: that ultra-clean room, the way her mother had seemed paralyzed with indecision, her father's insistence that Sabrina's disappearance didn't mean anything.

I instinctively knew that she'd never told them about the gang rape or any fears about being pregnant. She must have been terrified how they would react. She'd run away instead, assuming that living on the streets would be better than that. Who was I to say that she was wrong?

"Mom!" Joseph protested.

"She doesn't want to go home. It's clear she doesn't feel safe or accepted there. I don't know why, and that's not for me to say. For now, she's going to stay here." Because her other choice had been the streets of downtown Salt Lake City.

"Her parents don't deserve to be treated like this," Joseph said.

I looked over at Sabrina, who had her arms folded across her chest in a defensive stance. I didn't have any reason to think they had abused her. Maybe all they'd done was constantly criticize and rebuke. Sometimes, Mormonism made it almost seem like that was the only way to be a good parent. I regretted that any of my children might have ever felt a fraction of that.

"I've only been here a few hours," Sabrina said to Joseph. Her chin was high, though her voice was shaky. "And I can already tell you that these two strangers care about me more than my own parents. Your dad made me breakfast and asked what I wanted. And your mother made me a second breakfast and asked the same thing. Do you know that my parents have never done that for me, asked me what I wanted? Not once in my whole life. They were afraid the answers would be inconvenient for them."

Joseph looked stricken for a moment. "I'm sorry," he said.

She waved a hand. "No, don't be sorry. Being at your home with Carla, I got to pretend that I belonged there, too. That you and your wife loved me the way you loved her. That's why I always said yes. I'd cancel anything to come to your house. I wanted that feeling more than I wanted anything else in the world. Maybe that was why..." She stopped and started crying.

I wanted to reach for her and hold her tight, but I didn't have the chance.

"Excuse me," she said suddenly. "I'm tired and need some sleep."

"Of course," I said, unable to think of anything to counter that.

She didn't run up the stairs, but she went two at a time, swiftly and soundlessly in her bare feet.

Then I turned to Joseph.

"What am I supposed to do? Not tell her parents that she's okay? Mom, you have to know how they're feeling."

Did I? After what Sabrina had just said, I wasn't so sure. "She doesn't want to go home. She doesn't feel safe there."

"When charges are filed," Joseph said, "then she'll know people believe her."

I pinned him with a look. "And when will that happen?" I thought briefly of the recording I had, but I wasn't going to bring that up now. It wasn't in Sabrina's best interest.

He hesitated. "I don't know. I can't guarantee anything, but I talked to the police this morning."

"And what did they say?"

"They said—they took everything down. The list of names, the story, everything."

If Detective Gore were on this, I could accept that was enough. But I had no idea what the Ogden police force was like. I wondered if I could call her, if she could reach out to whoever would be on the case in Ogden. Maybe.

"Maybe we should accept that Sabrina knows what's best for her," I said. "She's had a very traumatic time. She probably needs to feel in control right now."

"Mom, she's a hormonal teenage girl. You can't let her make decisions about something like this."

Couldn't I? Just watch me, Joseph.

"I think she should go home to her parents," Joseph said firmly. "Where she belongs. Our ward can help her get through this. That's what the church is made for. This is what we do best. Helping people who need help."

As long as it was people who were hungry or who needed moving boxes packed into a van or weeds pulled out of an overgrown yard, I could agree with him. When it came to women who had suffered abuse, no, I didn't think that the Mormon Church had a good track record for helping there.

"You're not taking her back unless she decides she wants to go." I found my hands balled into fists, though I knew I wasn't about to get into a physical altercation with my own son.

Joseph sighed. "Mom, when I talked to the police, they asked me to tell them if I saw her or knew where she was. I can't keep this from them."

I positioned myself between Joseph and the stairs. "She's not leaving this house until she says she's ready."

"Mom, she needs help. Therapy. Maybe medication, too."

"She can get that here," I said.

"Without insurance?"

"If necessary," I said, knowing this was a bit unreasonable. But we had the money.

"Mom, if I don't tell her parents where she is, then I'm an accessory to a crime. You and Dad can be legally charged for harboring a runaway. Did you know that?" he demanded.

I wondered if Kurt had already thought about this. It was exactly the kind of thing he would have researched already, the minute he went to work.

Joseph moved toward the stairs, and I blocked him again, as ridiculous as it was for me to think I could physically stop him.

He stopped, looked down at me, and said, "Is this really what you want? For the police to come down here and force Sabrina home?"

He suddenly felt like a stranger to me. But I was the one who'd told him to talk to the police. And now it was coming back to haunt me. I'd thought I could use them to make sure I got the justice I wanted for Sabrina, forgetting that things didn't always work that way.

I relaxed and moved back toward the kitchen. He glanced up the stairs, then followed me. Good. We weren't at war, then.

"Give me some time," I said. If she could tell us more about what was going on at home, everyone could agree on next steps. Maybe her parents could go into therapy with her, though frankly I had a hard time imagining anyone being able to talk her father into something like that.

"Just a few days," I pleaded.

It was Christmastime, and Sabrina deserved to be happy and comfortable for the holidays. I was sure God had meant for it to be this way. For me to find her and bring her here, at least for a little while.

"She might be having a psychotic break. She could be dangerous," Joseph said.

What was he talking about? She'd said his home was the place she felt safest. She'd praised him to the skies, and he was calling her dangerous?

"I thought you were on her side," I said

Joseph raised his hands, then dropped them. "I am. But she's just a kid. She doesn't know what's best for her. She's upset at her parents, but she never told them anything. She didn't even give them the chance to help her."

Why was it always on the girls to do the work? "Give me one week with her before you tell the police."

"It's Christmas in a week," Joseph pointed out.

I was banking on that—providing her with one happy Christmas before having to deal with everything. "One week," I repeated.

In that week, I would get her to talk to me about what had made her run away when she did. I'd help her formulate some kind of plan to move forward, therapy or a youth shelter or something, anything besides going back on the streets. If she wanted to talk to the police and proceed with a trial, I'd give her all the support she needed.

Joseph walked out and got in his car, then drove back home. Probably after giving Kurt a quick earful about me on the phone from the driveway.

I made myself a burrito and ate it, only realizing afterward

I'd forgotten to put salsa on it. I packed everything else back up and put it in the fridge for Kurt to have later. Then I remembered in a panic: his suits at the dry cleaners. I rushed over and got there just in time. What would he have done without a Sunday suit? He couldn't show up to church in just a white shirt and tie, not as the bishop.

But no harm done. Maybe next time, I'd be better off bringing the suits in two batches, just in case.

Kurt got home late that night, and for the first time I could remember in the entire course of our marriage, he didn't come upstairs to our bedroom. I heard him settle himself on the couch downstairs and thought about taking him a blanket and pillow. But in the end, I decided that if he wanted to exile himself, he could do without the comforts a loving wife would normally have brought him.

CHAPTER 16

Sunday morning, I woke up in plenty of time to go to church. I even took a shower and got dressed, but I didn't walk over. I couldn't bear to leave Sabrina alone, let alone face the judgmental looks from Kurt. And I'd been telling myself for months now that it was time for me to take a sabbatical, get some distance from Mormonism and see if I still felt the same about it afterward. This seemed like the ideal opportunity, even a heaven-sent one.

So I went into the kitchen and started work on my traditional Christmas candy. I heard the shower going upstairs and then quiet for a while. Then I was preoccupied with my penuche fudge.

Most people make fudge with marshmallows and sweetened condensed milk, but I consider that the cheater's way out. Real fudge is just sugar and milk cooked to the right temperature, then beaten like a sinner in hell. I had my thermometer in the pan, waiting for it to cool to the right number, but I was also watching it like a hawk because I trusted my eye for fudge more than I trusted the thermometer, which might have told me just a minute too late. Sixty seconds is an eternity in fudge time.

I got out my spoon and started beating. I was dripping sweat in a couple of minutes. This was my best workout of the year. Other people did marathons; I did sweets.

When I was finished with the fudge, I checked my watch. It was 11 A.M., which meant Relief Society was starting. I felt a pang of guilt for not being there with the other sisters in my ward. How many calls would I get from people asking if I was sick or if they could do anything to help? That was both the perk and the pitfall of being the bishop's wife. Nothing you did or didn't do was invisible.

The penuche looked perfect in the pan, and I got out the walnut halves to decorate the top before I started cutting. I had caramel on the stove, but it still wasn't bubbling, so I didn't need to keep stirring. After that, I thought about what else I needed to do before Christmas. I hadn't gotten to the family letter yet, the one Kurt liked to send with our cards to ward members, family, and friends who'd moved away.

A family Christmas letter is always a tricky thing. You don't want to sound like you're bragging about how brilliant and accomplished your children are. But you also don't want to be too vague because the people you're sending the letter to are invested in your kids. They want to know what's going on. And talking about the kids was certainly easier than telling people I was questioning my place in Mormonism, that our marriage was in deep trouble, or about any of the cases in which I'd collided with the police this year.

Sabrina came down. "It smells great," she said with a flash of a smile.

I felt guilty immediately for doing something that must

seem trivial compared to everything that had happened to her. But maybe that was just what she needed.

"Candy making," I explained briefly. "Do you want me to whip you up something quick for breakfast?"

"Can I just sit and watch?" she asked.

I told her she could but felt self-conscious as she perched on the stool by the bar. I offered her a taste of the caramel at a couple of stages, less because I needed an opinion and more because I enjoyed the process of making caramel—and I wanted her to enjoy it, too. Caramel tasted good at every stage, but it could only be made into candy when it was just right.

"Do you need me to leave?" she asked quietly, as I was pouring the caramel out onto a greased cookie sheet.

"What? No. Just a minute." I put the empty pan back on the stove, set a timer, and turned back to her. I hadn't expected the abrupt question, especially because I'd tried to avoid the topic of her going home. "You're welcome to stay as long as you want."

She played with her hands. "Joseph doesn't seem very happy that I'm here. He and his family are the last people I want to cause problems for."

"They're fine. We talked about it last night, and he said you could stay until Christmas. We can figure things out after that," I said.

She played with her hair for a moment. "You said you found out about what happened with Jonathan and Pey—" She swallowed convulsively on the last syllable.

"Yes," I admitted. "Henry and Bella told me. They were worried about you."

She rubbed at her eyes. "Yeah. Henry and Bella are the best. My parents hate them because they're not Mormon, but they're the only ones who ever really cared about me."

I wondered for a brief moment whether Sabrina's frustration with her parents was teen angst, but I had to take her word for it. I wouldn't treat her like Joseph had last night— like she didn't know herself or what was best for her. "You can tell me about your parents, too."

She let out a short breath. "It's not like that," she said.

"Not like what?"

"They don't hit me or yell at me all the time or anything. They just don't . . ."

"Love you," I finished for her, remembering what she'd said last night.

She shrugged. "Maybe I'm not very lovable."

Anyone who made a girl her age feel like that earned my wrath, even if they hadn't intended it. "I'm sorry your parents have made you feel that way, Sabrina. Of course you deserve to be loved." I wanted to add something about God loving her infinitely, too, but I wasn't sure it was the right moment for that.

"I used to wonder if there were other kids in my family," she said.

I frowned, confused. "What do you mean?"

She shrugged. "Just that the way they talked, it seemed like there was a competition of some kind. They were holding me up to this pattern of a kid better than I was. Better in school and at church, more obedient. When I was little, I used to think they once had older kids that had already moved out or something. I did the math and figured out it was possible."

She looked very close to the edge of . . . something. "No one should make you feel inadequate. That isn't love," I said.

"They kept saying they were just helping me to be better. Didn't I want to be better?"

"Sabrina, I'm so sorry."

"And I *did* want to be better. So badly. But I never could do it enough for them to be happy. Eventually, I realized they were never going to love me. And when Jonathan and Peyton started paying attention to me, I just liked the way that they were both always there, looking at me like that. No one had ever looked at me like that. Maybe I should've picked one of them, like they asked. But I was afraid." She glanced up at me.

I nodded. I could understand why. "It's not your fault," I said.

"I mess up the lives of everyone around me. Everyone," she said. "That was why I left. I almost told Joseph about it. He was so nice to me. He seemed like someone who would understand. But then I remembered that even my own parents wouldn't understand."

"You're safe here," I said. It was clear to me now that I was in way over my head—I was no therapist. I'd thought bringing her home would be enough, but she needed more than what I could give her. I just wasn't sure she was ready for that right now.

"But now your husband . . ." She nodded at the couch, blankets folded neatly to one side.

"We'll be fine," I said. "Don't worry about that. We've been married for thirty years, and we're not going to split over one little fight that's mostly about me not answering his calls for a night." At least, I hoped not.

I caught the caramel bubbling again and went back to vigorously stirring. Maybe ordinary things like this could be good for both of us.

"Can I help?" she asked.

I didn't want to immediately initiate her into the highest levels of candy making, but Kurt often liked to volunteer, so I usually planned for something easy he could do.

"Chocolate pretzels?" I asked her. "I've got dipping chocolate and some choices for toppings."

"Great!" she said.

And the dipping chocolate could be worked in the microwave, which wouldn't interfere with my work on the stove.

I finished the caramel, poured it into an aluminum-foiled pan, and got out the dipping chocolate and pretzels for her and started on toffee myself.

A few minutes into that, I got a phone call. To my surprise, it wasn't Kurt. It was the new Relief Society president, Donna Ringel, who wanted to know if I was sick.

"I'm mostly just tired from holiday preparations," I said, prevaricating on telling her about my current doubts. If I did, there would be consequences, including people trying to either "fix" my problems or avoiding me for fear I might "contaminate" their testimonies. Not to mention, yet again, the threat of Kurt being released as bishop if his wife wasn't the stellar example of Mormon womanhood that leadership wanted. He'd never forgive me if that happened.

"Don't worry about me," I added.

"All right, then. You take care."

I hung up and turned back to see that Sabrina had chocolate up to her elbows, as well as spattered all over her face and the pajamas I'd given her. But she seemed to be having a good time, so I didn't say anything. She had a long piece of waxed paper stretched out on the dining room table that she was covering with finished pretzels, dotted with red and green sprinkles, coconut, and chopped pecans.

In the midst of this, there was a loud knock on the front door. Joseph again?

I looked at my hands, sticky and spotted with candy, grabbed a towel and headed to the door to try to open it cleanly.

But it wasn't Joseph. This time, it was a man dressed in a heavy coat with work gloves on. He was about five foot eight but wiry and strong-looking. I guessed he was about fifty years old. I didn't recognize him, but his eyes narrowed at the sight of me.

"Where's my daughter?" he demanded in a voice I recognized from our phone call.

"Mr. Jensen?" I said.

"Where's Sabrina?" he said again.

Had Joseph told him Sabrina was here? I thought I'd made it pretty clear to him not to do that.

"I don't know what you're talking about," I stonewalled, hoping Sabrina wouldn't wander in from the kitchen.

"I called your son last night, and he told me not to worry about Sabrina. He said you'd spoken to her and she was fine. I asked him where she was and when she was coming home where she belonged, but he wouldn't say anything more. And that's when I knew where she was. So I looked up your address online and drove down here. Now, where's my daughter?"

The way he said it made her sound like a possession he'd lost or like a stray pet. I found myself feeling even more certain about my choice not to send her home.

"She's not here," I said, setting my jaw.

"Why should I believe you?" he asked.

"Because I'm telling you the truth," I lied, feeling no moral compunction about it. "I saw her downtown near Pioneer Park last night. I talked to her for a few minutes, and she seemed fine. That's all I told Joseph."

He didn't react for a moment. "Pioneer Park?" he said, after a beat.

I nodded. This was going to work. "It's on 400 West, right off the freeway. Maybe if you go there tonight you can find her yourself."

"Tonight? Why would I wait for tonight?"

"Sometimes they go to other places during the day. I don't know if she'll be there now," I said, not mentioning the library.

His eyes narrowed. "You're sure she was there?" he asked.

"Yes. I talked to her. She said she didn't want to come home yet. But she seemed in good spirits otherwise. I gave her some food I'd brought with me. Granola bars, things like that. Water." I hoped this would work—and quickly.

"And you didn't bring her back?" he asked.

"I would've tried, but she was too jumpy. Besides, it's not like she knows me," I said. Looking into the face of this angry man, I recommitted to my story.

"Well, that girl has been a trial since the day she was born. They say that being a parent is the hardest work you'll ever do, but for me and Rae, it's been the most thankless, too. She has no gratitude, no sense of what we've given up for her. It's always about her, about what she needs, never any sacrifice for the family she owes everything to."

"Well, they say trials refine us," I said, mostly to the empty air as he turned away without saying goodbye, headed back to his truck.

I closed the door, breathing deeply and trying not to feel faint. I stayed there until I could hear the engine driving off. Even then, I was afraid. I stepped back out and looked up and down the street. I didn't see anyone, but I locked the front door when I came back in.

"Sabrina?" I called as I walked into the kitchen. She wasn't there. Where had she gone?

I hustled upstairs, my heart thumping loudly with the fear that she'd left through a window. She wasn't in Zachary's room. Or the bathroom. I tried all the other bedrooms upstairs, including my own. I was about to call Joseph to give him a piece of my mind when it occurred to me to check the basement. She'd gone down there to get food for dinner last night. Maybe she'd tried to hide there.

I opened the door and called out, "Sabrina? It's me. Linda. Your father's gone. You don't have to worry. I told him you were still downtown." I flicked on the light and walked cautiously down the stairs.

I found Sabrina crouched near the rows of cans, holding one high above her head like she was ready to launch it. A defensive weapon?

"You okay?" I asked.

"He's really gone?" she said, her eyes slowly focusing on me.

I nodded and held out my hand for the can of olives.

She gave it to me and stood back up. She was shaking again, just like last night.

"Do you want to come back up?" I asked.

She followed up. "I was sure you'd show him in. I thought you'd make me go home with him."

She needed professional help, that was certain. But not right now. Right now, it seemed that what she needed most was safety. And maybe some harmless fun. "Are you done with those pretzels?" I asked.

She nodded.

"You want a sandwich?"

She nodded again, and I made her a tuna salad sandwich. She nibbled at it, and when she was finished, she said she was tired again and disappeared back upstairs.

I made divinity, but I overcooked the syrup and had to throw it all out. Kurt came home about thirty minutes later.

"You're back early," I said softly.

"I canceled the rest of the tithing settlement appointments for day. My clerk will have to reschedule them for later this week."

I was tense, sure he would blame me outright for making him unable to focus on his work. "Do you want something to eat?"

"Thank you," he said hoarsely.

Neither of us spoke as I made him a sandwich just like the one I'd made Sabrina. I realized I was going to have to get used to having a third person in the house after being in an empty nest for more than a year. Should I suggest we go into Kurt's office to talk, or was she already sound asleep? I hoped we wouldn't start yelling and wake her.

"I'm sorry," I said.

Kurt looked up from the last bite of his sandwich. "It's not you, Linda," he said. "I mean, I'm angry with you for lying to me and for endangering yourself out on the streets all night. But I suppose I should be getting used to it by now. This is the new you." He motioned with his hand at me from head to toe.

"You've never slept on the couch before," I said, surprised at the catch in my voice.

"I wasn't really sleeping. I was tossing and turning, and I didn't want to wake you up after everything you went through the night before." He paused. "Besides, I was afraid I would take it out on you and start shouting at you about something that wasn't really your fault."

Not my fault. Then he didn't mean Sabrina. I had a tendency to think everything wrong in Kurt's life had to do with me. It was self-centered, and our therapist had noted it.

"The family in the ward who called on Monday?" I asked, even though I knew he still couldn't really tell me anything.

"It's so terrible," he said, shaking his head. His eyes were already red, but now they filled with tears that ran down his cheeks unchecked. He sobbed, and I put out my arms. He seemed to fall right into them.

"It's not your fault," I said. I seemed to be saying that a lot lately.

"I know that," he said brokenly. "But I just don't know how anyone can fix a problem so deep and so wide."

"You always say to go to Jesus when it seems like it's too big." I might have questioned Mormonism, but my faith in Christ was firm as ever, maybe more so.

"Yeah." He sniffed. "Maybe when everyone is dead, that will help. But for now, Jesus isn't going to make all of this go away."

For Kurt to admit that was pretty sad.

"Do you want some penuche fudge?" I asked lamely.

He let out a rough laugh. "Actually, you know what? I do."

I went and got him a plate.

He ate two pieces, which was more than he usually had in one sitting, since he'd never had much of a sweet tooth. Then he asked if he could help me with the family Christmas letter. I told him my ideas, and to my surprise, he brought his laptop into the kitchen and started working on it. Within an hour, we had something ready to print.

After that, we turned on *Longmire*, Kurt's favorite mystery show. I suspected he sometimes imagined himself as Walt Longmire, the sheriff in a small Wyoming town—not much for talking, but smart and loyal and ready to do what was right, no matter what it took. I was no Katee Sackhoff, but I liked the show anyway.

Sabrina snuck down and sat on the other side of the couch, knees up to her chest, arms wrapped around them for the second episode. She didn't say a word, but I felt her glancing at Kurt more than once. Maybe she saw the Longmire in him, too; I wasn't sure. There were certain advantages to being a sheriff over being a Mormon bishop. You could put the bad guys in jail and get rid of them without anyone else's permission, for one. But in a ward, the bad guys never really went away. And you were supposed to try to save everyone.

CHAPTER 17

The next morning, I packed Kurt a lunch of the leftover burritos he'd missed two days before and talked to him about my plans for the day with Sabrina. Putting aside the big emotional and psychological needs to deal with later, I decided to focus on the physical. I needed to get her some clothes that fit her properly, and I thought about taking her to the mall to grab a few things while I finished up my Christmas shopping.

"What's the story with her parents? I thought you and Joseph agreed they weren't abusive. Why isn't she back at home?" Kurt asked.

Sometimes it was hard to get Kurt to engage on a deeper emotional level.

"She doesn't want to go home," I said. That should have been enough for both of us.

"I know she thinks that, but she's a teenager. Surely we should encourage her to trust the adults in her life."

Kurt hadn't heard her talk about how much she longed for a home like Joseph's—or ours. It was strange to think that with all the problems Kurt and I had, the sense of near-constant agitation between us, Sabrina still thought that we were more loving than her own parents. That spoke volumes to me. I wasn't about to push her away, not when she needed us most.

"Teenager or not, Sabrina isn't a piece of property. She's a person, and she should be able to make a choice about where she feels safe," I said.

He let a frustrated breath out. "You're not thinking clearly here. You're already too emotionally involved."

Right. I was a woman, so I was by default too emotional. I said through clenched teeth, "She's a vulnerable girl who needs to be treated with kid gloves until she's ready to talk about it. If we try to force her back home, she'll just bolt again and end up on the streets for good. Is that what you want?" Was that logical enough for him? What I really wanted to say was, *Believe women.* Even when they were fifteen and struggling. But Kurt would never see this as I did.

"Linda, I know you think you're responsible for her because you found her, but she's not your child," Kurt said.

I gaped at him. This wasn't about me. This was about Sabrina. "Kurt, Sabrina is the victim of a gang rape," I said, refusing to mince my words. How was I the only adult in her life who cared about the repercussions of that?

Kurt put up his hands. "I know. She needs to see a therapist. But first she should be home with her parents. They need to be the ones help get her through this. It's their responsibility and their *right*, Linda. Can you imagine how you would feel if one of our sons ran away and someone else took him in, tried to take our place, and lied to us about it? You'd be ready to bring one of my guns along."

I flinched at that. Kurt and the boys went hunting every fall, but he kept all the guns locked in the basement, and I never cared to see them. Kurt sent out the meat to be cleaned and cut by a professional, so all I had to do was find recipes for venison.

"It's not the same," I said. "It's not the same at all. You haven't met the Jensens. They aren't paying attention. They don't make her feel loved."

"So because they're not parenting the way you think they should, they get their parenting card revoked? Linda, that's not fair."

I swallowed and sobered a little. Kurt had a point, and I knew his intentions were good. "Look, this is just a temporary solution. Joseph says he'll call her parents on Christmas. If Sabrina says she's ready to go home before that, I'll gladly drive her to Ogden. But until then, I think you should spend a little time with her and gauge what she needs. All right?" I wished our own marriage counselor could mediate this for us but knew the situation would stay inside this household.

Kurt sighed and ran a hand through his thinning hair. "I'll pray about her, Linda. But that's all I can promise."

"Fine," I said, though I worried the answer to his prayer would just be more of the same. How easy it was to get answers from God that confirmed your own biases. I was starting to be more and more aware of that.

Kurt turned back. "Linda, I know it's hard for you now that Samuel is gone and you're at home alone," he said gently.

I rolled my eyes. "Kurt, this is not about me being a bored housewife." How dare he accuse me of that.

He rolled his eyes. "Bored housewife? Linda, you are the

last woman on Earth who would ever be bored. What I mean is that you want to be *needed*. You want to do things that matter. You're trying to save this girl," he said.

Okay, true. But what was so wrong with that?

"Last year, you told me you wanted me to think about fostering and even adopting older children, and I know I haven't been very welcoming to the idea," Kurt said.

That was an understatement. He'd completely nixed it until he was released as bishop. He'd said that before then he had too much "on his plate." And I had asked him, what about me? Why did what *I* wanted not matter?

"I think you should take my time as bishop as a chance to rest and relax, not make your life more complicated," he'd said. He meant make *his* life more complicated, and it had been the best I could do then not to hit him over the head with a pot. What he was really saying was that while he was bishop, I was supposed to be in a holding pattern, circling around him and his calling.

"I'm not doing this as some kind of workaround," I insisted. And I wasn't. Or at least, not intentionally. I hadn't asked for Sabrina to be part of our lives. Joseph had dragged me into this, and after that, I'd only done what I'd felt was right.

"Well, that's what it looks like from here," Kurt said.

"Oh, really? You think I'm trying to adopt a teenager whose parents want her back? You must think I'm stupid as well as selfish, then, because even having her in the house could get me arrested."

"That's exactly my point," Kurt said.

"That I'm stupid?" I challenged. I wasn't backing down on this, not even for Kurt.

"No, Linda. That you're not thinking clearly. This girl already has parents. You can't be her mother. You're just going to end up getting hurt in all of this. You have this big heart, and you want to give and give to people. But it's not always the right thing to do."

"Right, I think Jesus said that. He said give until it's not convenient to give anymore, for such is the kingdom of heaven," I retorted.

Kurt took in a deep breath and held it for several beats. "You're not listening," he said.

"Neither are you." I was the one who had stayed out in the freezing cold all night to find Sabrina Jensen. Not Kurt. Not Joseph. Not even her own parents. And if I tried to send her home, she was going to head straight back to the streets, and who knew what could happen to her there? I was trying to protect her, not become her mother.

"Linda, she isn't Georgia," Kurt said.

I let those words fall slowly and splinter into pieces like glass on the cement.

Then I walked out of the garage and didn't look back.

CHAPTER 18

When Kurt and I were first married, we'd gotten into a lot of arguments. About the church: its treatment of women, its politics, its history. You name it, we fought over it. But we never yelled. It wasn't a rule we'd made consciously—it was just that neither Kurt nor I were yellers. We were both stewers, letting anger fester within.

We both habitually cleaned our frustrations away. So when the house was sparkling and neat was when we were twitching with the need to keep our mouths shut. When the house was dirty, we were getting along.

After Kurt left, I got down on my hands and knees and used a kitchen towel to wipe the floor from end to end. You never really got it clean with a regular mop, not to mention those ridiculous Swiffer cleaning "solutions" that cost a hundred dollars and didn't make a dent in five sons' worth of kitchen dirt. Hands and knees, just like Cinderella in every movie iteration, that was how to really clean a kitchen floor. I could feel the ache in my back, the heat in my shoulders and arms, and the sting of my knees as skin broke open and bled onto my pants. It felt good to me. Like a sacrifice on the altar of life.

When I was done with the floor, I started in on the refrigerator. I sighed at my problem with leftovers. I tended to keep everything because you never knew when one of the boys might stop in and decide he was starving and needed that last serving of pot pie from the night before. But now, the boys weren't stopping in from high school sports or even college to grab meals anymore. Kurt took leftovers to work sometimes but not often. As for me, well, I'd never eat a day-old meal if I could make a fresh one.

The refrigerator was full of things that had been in there too long, and by the time I was finished with the inside, I had a stack of Tupperware containers to deal with. Cleaning them out took another hour. By then, I was exhausted and ready to take a nap. But climbing into our bed by myself would only remind me of Kurt, and I didn't want that. I wanted to keep working.

I started a new batch of toffee after the cleaning was done. I didn't mean for it to be my lunch, but the timing meant it was.

Sabrina came downstairs right after I'd poured the hot candy into a pan and sprinkled chocolate chips and chopped pecans on top.

"Want some?" I asked her, offering her the bowl. The boys had always liked chipping at toffee, licking at the wooden spoon, letting the pan cool in their hands.

Sabrina shook her head. "It looks good, but could I have some milk and cereal instead?"

Again? What was it with her and cereal?

But I gestured to the cabinet where the cereal boxes were, since my hands were still sticky.

She asked me if I wanted anything, but I was already full of toffee, the lunch of champion Christmas bakers.

"I don't suppose you have any coffee?" she asked as she pulled a clean bowl and spoon from the dishwasher.

"No," I said a little wistfully.

"Yeah, my parents never had it in the house, either. I had to sneak it."

So I could've ordered a cup at that drive-through after all. I thought about how to frame my next question the right way but couldn't think of one.

"Do you . . . still consider yourself a Mormon?" I asked. Maybe it self-serving to ask, since I was in the midst of my own doubts.

Sabrina tensed. "I don't know. I don't think I fit in anymore."

I understood that feeling only too well and had since I'd been just a few years older than Sabrina, when my first husband had come out and we'd gotten divorced. Right now, she needed someone to tell her that she could move forward after this.

"Do you still believe in God?" I asked quietly.

She considered this for a long moment. "I guess I do, only He's a sadistic bastard if He let this happen or thought I deserved it."

"That's not what God thinks," I said fiercely. "God loves you just as much as He ever did, and I promise you, it's those boys He's angry at."

She shrugged, unwilling to talk directly about what had happened.

I sighed and let her finish her cereal. "We could go out for coffee, if you want. There's a Starbucks nearby," I offered.

She made a face.

"What's wrong?"

"Starbucks is kind of boring, you know. Any better local coffee places?" she asked.

"I actually don't know," I said. I'd been out for coffee with Gwen Ferris, but it had always been in Orem, where she was finishing classes at the police academy. I'd been nervous about anyone so close to home seeing their bishop's wife getting coffee in public. "I'm sure we could find one."

Sabrina seemed a little more animated now, which had to be a good thing. "Fine, we can do Starbucks. I think it'll help me feel more alive."

"And after that? Maybe some lunch? Or Christmas shopping?" I asked her. Mine was mostly done, but the sales were so good that I let myself buy things that weren't necessarily for Christmas, too.

She stared at me blankly. "I don't have any money," she said. Which didn't necessarily mean she didn't want to buy gifts.

I'd tell Kurt that this was a step toward her heading home, eventually. She could buy presents for her parents, for Henry and Bella. It would remind her of her relationships with them, and maybe she'd want to go home on her own in time.

"My treat," I said. "If you see something you want for yourself or anyone else, I'll get it for you."

After a quick stop at Starbucks, which she didn't seem as unhappy about as she'd pretended, we went to the South Towne mall. It was so packed that we had to park in the far end of the parking lot to the east of the sprawling complex itself.

Inside it was warm, at least. Plenty of bodies added to the heat pumping through the vents, along with the sound of canned, cheesy Christmas music that was supposed to elicit the Pavlovian response of making us spend. Press Play on Bing Crosby singing "White Christmas," add ten percent to your day's profit.

"Shop first, lunch after?" I asked.

Sabrina shrugged.

I dragged her to every clothing store I could think of and bought her a new coat that was rated for weather below fifteen degrees, new boots, new gloves, a scarf, and a hat—the kind you couldn't knit yourself. Also new wool socks.

These were just everyday necessities, though, and I wanted her to have something fun. So when we passed a jewelry shop, I asked her if she wanted anything.

She wouldn't even go in. "That's just stuff for people to steal. Anything they can take, they can sell; it's so easy."

I didn't ask where she'd learned this rule of commerce. I tried to suppress the thought of her going back to Missy's group.

We passed a Lovesac store, and I convinced her to come in with me and test out one of the pod couches. "Wouldn't this be great to sit on while watching TV?" I asked, though I was pretty sure Kurt would want nothing to do with Love-related furniture. He liked his couches more traditionally designed.

"I don't understand why people would spend that much money on basically a sack filled with foam," Sabrina said as we walked out.

I wondered if this frugality was because her parents had struggled financially or something more newfound from her recent days away from home, living on much less.

Later, I got Sabrina to sample some of the Hickory Farms

display out in the middle of the mall. She tasted it and nodded. "I like it." She sounded surprised. Had she never had Hickory Farms before?

I got her one of the gift boxes, despite her complaints that it was too expensive, and we moved on.

Then we found a board game shop at the end of the mall, and I told her I wanted to go in and look for something for Kurt even though I'd already bought a Christmas present for him. Once upon a time, Kurt had fancied himself a grand board-game master. He and I had courted over Risk and gone through stages Othello, Go, and Chaos in our marriage. Then the kids came, and we moved to Chutes and Ladders, Monopoly Junior, and LIFE.

But I hadn't seen Kurt play an actual board game for years. Being the bishop hadn't given him any time for it, and even before that, he'd been Scoutmaster, which meant most of his free time was related to camping or the merit badges required for an Eagle.

"I'd like to get something for my husband," I told Sabrina. The thought made me almost giddy, bringing back so many fond memories of our courtship.

I was surprised at how many games I found that looked like they could work. I got one called Cathedral for Kurt with wooden pieces that resembled churches. It seemed appropriate, given his calling, and it looked like it was both simple enough to learn in a night and complex enough to remain interesting for years on end.

I also found a game for each of my sons except Samuel, who wouldn't be able to play it on his mission. Every minute was scheduled and meant to be "given to God."

"Do you think I could get this?" asked Sabrina, showing me a three-pack of playing cards.

I thought at first that she wanted them because of the photos on the back, which were of the male leads of the new *Star Trek* series in provocative poses. "You like *Star Trek*?" I asked.

She gave me a blank look. "Huh?"

I didn't bother getting into it. "Do they have any other sets? If you just want the cards, that is."

She nodded in the direction of the shelf where she'd found them. "I didn't see any others."

We took the cards to the desk along with the board games I'd picked out, and I asked if they had other playing card sets. They showed us the standard ones behind the desk, which were a little cheaper and could be purchased as singles.

"How many decks do you want?" I asked Sabrina.

She chewed at her lower lip. "Can I get three?" she asked finally.

I paused. "Three it is," I said, and we were carrying so many bags I wished for the days when I had pushed a stroller around the mall. Sabrina was carrying several already, but she had to take another or I wouldn't be able to walk upright. I looked around for a cart and finally found one we could rent for ten dollars. It seemed outrageous, but I paid it anyway, just to save my back, which had been complaining angrily since my overnight adventure in the cold on Friday.

"Ready for a late lunch?" I asked. We were on the opposite side of the mall from the car, but we could drop off everything there, lock it, and go to one of the restaurants around the edge. My vote was for Mimi's Cafe because it had what I thought of as comfort food. Mashed potatoes, biscuits with gravy, and steaks covered with mushrooms.

But when we got back to the car, Sabrina asked if there was a buffet place we could go to so she could try lots of different things. We ended up at the Golden Corral just across the parking lot.

Sabrina piled her tray high with salad fixings that looked like they might weigh more than she did.

I didn't protest but was curious to watch and see how much she could actually finish. To my surprise, she ate it all and went back for a fourth plate of breads and soups, then had dessert, as well.

She finally got herself a big soup bowl of ice cream with lots of caramel sauce and sprinkles. "While you're staying with us, I want you to feel at home. You can invite friends over, if you want. Henry and Bella, maybe?" I asked.

She tensed, and I realized I had hit on a touchy subject. "No, thank you," she said.

I knew this wasn't the time to talk about heavy stuff, not when we were in public. I cursed my timing. "Well, anything I can do to help," I said. "Just say the word."

She was silent for a long moment, then started tapping the table. "I don't know," she said. "You've already spent a lot on me. I don't think it's fair for me to ask for more."

Now I was getting excited. "Oh, don't worry. Kurt makes a good living, and I don't have anyone else to spend on nowadays, really."

"What about your kids?" Sabrina said. "And grandkids?"

I pointed to the packages around us. "I think they have plenty."

She looked down and kept talking. "You know, I started working with my father when I was six or seven. He paid me ten cents an hour, and I thought it was so cool. I had my own money to spend. But then they expected me to buy most things on my own. Clothes, school things, activities with friends—if my parents let me go with them at all. I took everything I'd saved with me when I left, but it still wasn't enough to buy what I wanted."

I spoke cautiously. "Sometimes you have to wait until you're older to get those things. I wish it weren't true, but for me, it helped to think that I could give more to my children than my parents gave to me."

It was the wrong thing to say. Sabrina flinched as if I had hit her, then looked away, emotional walls back up.

I drove her home and took her things into Zachary's room.

"Can I ask you something?" she said, when my hand was on the doorknob.

"Sure. Of course," I said.

"Do you think God can forgive anything?"

Was this about what happened to her? It still brought on a physical ache that she thought of it as something *she* had somehow done.

"I think God's capacity to love is infinite," I said softly. A warmth filled me, and not just my own. I was ready to hug her and pat her back.

But her face froze, and she put her hands to her cheeks. "I don't think I want God, then," she said and turned her back to me.

I walked out of the room and downstairs to the living room, collapsing onto the couch. So she hadn't meant herself but the young men who had committed an unforgivable crime. Maybe I wasn't prepared to have Sabrina here after all, as I seemed to take every wrong step in these conversations.

Should I be praying for vengeance on those boys? I understood her point of view, having felt it myself a few times after the cases I'd been involved in. I wondered if that was why my views of Mormonism were changing so rapidly: because I'd been face to face with real evil and didn't feel as far from it as I had before.

Before I forgot, I had to call Detective Gore. I stepped out on the back porch and dialed. When she picked up, I hurriedly explained Sabrina's complicated situation, from the gang rape to her running away from home to live on the streets.

"Now, how exactly are you involved in this, Mrs. Wallheim?" she asked.

"My son Joseph is in her ward. She babysat his daughter a lot," I explained.

"Ah. I knew there would be a connection. Mormons are like octopuses with a thousand arms—they've got people in every city."

"Uh, yes, I suppose that's true. It's easy to connect." The church hadn't been very global before the '80s but had become very much so since then. But we were getting off track.

"Is there anything you can do to help her? Call the police in Ogden? Tell them that they should believe her, or put pressure on them to make arrests?"

There was a long silence during which I began to worry that I'd offended her. It wasn't what I'd intended to do, but I seemed to say the wrong thing to her so much of the time. It was a wonder she had taken my call in the first place.

"No, I can't put pressure on colleagues in another department to make an arrest if they don't see the evidence for it," she said precisely.

"I see."

"She'd have to go be interviewed. Any other witnesses would have to speak. Then they'd have to talk to the boys involved, as well," Gore said.

I'd assumed as much. "Will you tell me what you think the chances are that there would be a conviction? That they'd serve any time at all?"

She hesitated.

"It's because they're good Mormon boys," I said. "Is that it?"

"Rape cases are difficult to prosecute all over the country, regardless of religion," Gore said. "The real problem is that she's waited so long."

I bristled at that. So it was her fault that she'd been intimidated and threatened by her attackers?

"But she should do it anyway," Gore said. "If more victims came forward, it would help the whole system to begin to normalize the process and for people in general to stop making excuses for rapists."

I digested this for a moment. "So you're saying she should do it because it will help future victims. Not because she's likely to get justice for herself."

Gore cleared her throat. "I'm sorry, Mrs. Wallheim," she said. "I can't change the world for you. Or for her."

And that, as they say, was that.

I hung up, feeling sick inside, and had to remind myself not to mention anything about this conversation to Sabrina.

CHAPTER 19

"I took Sabrina shopping for winter stuff," I said when Kurt got home.

"She probably has all that at home, you know," Kurt said.

"I don't think so," I said, remembering her closet. For all the nice clothes she'd left behind, I hadn't seen a heavy coat.

"Is she still here?" he asked, looking around.

"She's upstairs," I said, nodding upward.

"Are we doing Family Home Evening tonight?" he asked.

I thought about it, but not for very long. "I'll ask Sabrina after dinner, all right?" I said. I didn't want to put pressure on her if she didn't want to, but maybe it would distract her for a little while if we played games.

Kurt shrugged, and we worked on dinner together for a bit. It was nice to know that even after arguments, our kitchen rhythm was much the same. He could still chop up vegetables for a salad and set a table without once getting in my way. We were having one of my best dishes: beef stew that I'd put in the Crock-Pot before shopping.

I went upstairs to get Sabrina. For a brief moment, looking into Zachary's room, I thought she'd disappeared. There was no sign of her. The bags and packages we'd bought earlier that day weren't anywhere I could see. The window was open, despite the winter cold pouring through, and I poked my head out to look down at the short drop from the roof to the ground. She could have left that way. Then where would she go?

"Mrs. Wallheim?" I heard behind me.

I nearly decapitated myself as I tried to pull my head back inside.

"I was just in the bathroom," Sabrina was saying when I turned to face her.

"Why did you open the window?"

She shrugged. "I was a little hot, and I kind of wanted fresh air."

"It's freezing outside," I said, biting my tongue to avoid mention of the heating bill.

"I know, but it smells good—natural, somehow. I mean, like the mountains. Not like the city."

That came from us living so high up and from being far enough from the pollution of the rest of the valley.

"Dinner's ready. I hope you like beef stew."

"Sure," she said and came downstairs. Her eyes lit up when she saw the Crock-Pot. "Homemade?" She sounded like she'd never had such a thing. She also ate amounts rivaling our buffet experience.

Then she sat back with what looked like a real smile on her face. "I should have guessed Brother Wallheim's parents would be just as awesome as he is, but I never knew a family could be like this."

I felt terrible because it didn't seem like we'd even done

anything special. She was just happy to be eating a regular dinner on a Monday night.

"Want to play a board game with us?" Kurt asked before I had the chance to bring up the question of Family Home Evening.

"You play games?" Sabrina asked, surprised.

"What? You think we're too old for games?" Kurt shot back at her.

It was the first time they'd engaged, and I was tense for a moment.

"Not too old," Sabrina said.

"Oh, too boring, then," Kurt said, teasing. "We don't like fun. We just work and eat all the time. And then sit around in our spare time?"

I nudged Kurt, thinking he'd gone too far.

But Sabrina laughed. "What kind of games do you have?"

Kurt took her over to the game cupboard, which was handily at the bottom of my china cabinet, where the boys had insisted on putting them years ago when we all admitted that the china wasn't going to be coming out nearly as often as the games.

They talked over different possibilities and ended up deciding on Trains, which Sabrina said she'd never heard of before and Kurt promised would be easy to learn but still challenging. He set out the cards and explained it to her.

And then we both discovered what a cutthroat game player she was. Every time she got more points or more money, she gloated and showed us how far she was ahead of us. Kurt tried to give her a run for her money, but it was useless. She took over the whole board by the end.

"I guess we are too old for games, after all," he said.

"I guess you are," Sabrina agreed.

"Or too boring," Kurt added.

Sabrina put up her hands. "I didn't say that!" she insisted.

Before Kurt could respond to her, his phone rang. Sabrina jumped a bit, but Kurt stood up and looked an apology at me. Then he pulled the phone out of his pocket and said, "Hello?" He then made a series of noncommittal noises that indicated it was a bishop call.

"Do your parents ever play board games with you?" I asked, trying to keep it casual.

She froze a moment. "No," she said simply.

"Oh. Some people just aren't board game people."

"My parents definitely aren't board game people," she said.

There was a long pause as we put the cards away. Then I took the game back to the cabinet. When I came back, Sabrina said, "You know, I've never seen a family that does this."

"Play board games?" I asked, confused.

"Yes. Play board games and buy clothes for no reason and cook homemade beef stew and just . . ." She waved around the room. "No yelling. No anger. No fear."

We were getting into real stuff here, and I didn't know what to say. I wanted her to keep talking but only if it made her feel safer. "We're just a regular family," I said.

"No, you're not," she said sharply.

I still didn't know what her home life had been like, for her to decide that living on the streets was better. But even if there hadn't been any physical abuse, it had to have been pretty bad if she thought that Kurt and me playing Trains was so great.

I thought again about the apostle who had said in a recent conference that even if you didn't believe Mormonism was true, wasn't it a great way to live your life? Didn't it make people happy and keep families together? I'd been so angry at the time because I had heard from Samuel about friends of his who didn't have any relationship with their parents at all because of their sexual orientation. I'd blamed Mormonism for that, but maybe that wasn't entirely fair. Maybe there were things that I'd sorely miss if I let it go completely.

"If you want to play again tomorrow night, we can," I said.

Sabrina looked over to Kurt through the doorway of his bishop office at his desk, hunched over with the responsibility of trying to fix an impossible problem.

"It must be hard with people calling him all the time, asking for help," she said.

"Yes," I said. "It is."

"But it's like you're lending him to them. I think that's nice. Sharing family. You're doing it for me, too. I see that," she said. Then she headed upstairs, her arms folded around her stomach in a self-protective gesture.

My own parents hadn't been great while I was growing up, and I'd always promised myself that I'd do better by my kids. And I had. I knew that. But there were always problems. I just hadn't banked on someone reminding me of their scale.

I cleaned up the kitchen and started the dishwasher, then checked in with Kurt in his office before heading to bed myself. He had his hands folded across his chest and was staring at the painting of Christ in the Garden of Gethsemane with the archangel Michael behind him, an expression of pain, exhaustion, and overwhelming despair on his face. The painting was by James Christensen, but it might as well have been a mirror of Kurt's own countenance.

"I'm so sorry," I said. "I don't know what's happened, but I'm sorry." He deserved my care. Sabrina's opinion of him was right: he was a good man, and I was sharing him with people who needed him.

He let out a long sigh. "Well, there's not much point in keeping it secret now. The truth will be everywhere by morning."

It wasn't just curiosity that made me ask, "That means you can tell me?"

"At least part of it. Trevor Amos is coming home tonight."

Trevor Amos had just left on his mission two weeks before. "Isn't he still in the MTC?" I asked.

Kurt nodded, lips pressed to bloodlessness.

"Is he ill?" I asked.

"Not in any physical way," Kurt said.

"Did he . . . come out?" I asked, feeling a pang at the thought of Samuel, who was struggling so much with his own place in the Mormon Church, being openly gay and trying to serve a mission even when those around him thought his very essence evil.

Kurt shook his head, his expression grim.

"Did he admit to some kind of sexual indiscretion at the MTC? One that he hadn't confessed before?" I asked.

Kurt said nothing, just sat still staring at the painting just beyond me, so I suspected I'd hit the nail on the head.

"You feel responsible for this somehow?" I asked.

"I'm the bishop. I should be inspired to know if someone is worthy or not. Or if there are problems they haven't mentioned to me."

Ideally, I supposed this was true. But in real life, that level of discernment seemed an impossible bar.

"Well, bed sounds pretty good right now. We've both had a full day," I said, hoping he would say he would come with me. He didn't.

I checked on Sabrina on my way to bed. She still had the window open in her room. "Are you sure you don't want to close it?" I asked, trying to leave the choice to her. "It's going to get pretty cold overnight."

She was tucked up to her neck in double blankets and smiled. "I'll be fine. If it's too much, I'll get up and close it, but for now, I like it."

I tried not to interpret this as her liking the idea that she could escape anytime she wanted to. But I wasn't her jailer, and this house wasn't her prison. The only way I was really going to help her was to make sure she knew she was safe, that she could be part of the family life she seemed to like so much.

I was ready to fall into bed, but then I had an idea. I texted Gwen to see if she was awake, and when she said she was, I went into the bathroom to talk to her. Two doors between me and Sabrina seemed enough.

"Good to hear from you, Linda. What's up?"

I explained briefly about Sabrina staying with us.

"So you finally have your daughter," Gwen said.

It annoyed me that this sounded so much like what Kurt had said. "She's not my daughter. She's a fifteen-year-old who was gang-raped by a group of Mormon boys in her own ward," I blurted out.

Gwen was silent for a moment. Then I heard her burst out into tears.

God, what had I been thinking, saying that so callously? I'd wanted her advice because she was in the police academy, but she'd been sexually abused throughout her childhood by her father, and I hadn't meant to bring it up like that.

"I'm sorry, Gwen. I should have asked if you were in a good space to listen to something like this first."

She went on sobbing.

"Listen, this isn't your problem. I can call back later." I wanted to comfort her, too, but wanted to give her the option of processing this alone.

"No, Linda," she said softly. A deep breath, and then, "Just give me a minute."

I gave her several.

"You really have a way with words, you know that?" she said and gave a hiccupping laugh-sob.

"My gift," I said sarcastically.

"Has she talked to the police?" Gwen asked.

"No," I said. I explained that, too, and about the recording I had. And about my call to Detective Gore. "Should I tell her about any of that?"

"Don't pressure her. It has to be her choice if she wants to try to prosecute. A trial will be horrible. You can't sugarcoat that part. Do you think she's up for it?"

Before today, I'd have said no. But seeing her regain her strength and hearing her insight on family and forgiveness, maybe I'd underestimated her. "Possibly, in time," I said.

"All right," Gwen said. "In the meantime, you have to make sure she has the final say on everything that matters in her life. Do you understand? Control has been taken from her in a terrible way. She may have trouble trusting people. She may test you, to see if you'll still accept her."

"Test me how?" I asked.

"Say cruel things. Steal things. I don't know. It depends on the kid. In my teens, I slept with the guys my father would most hate me sleeping with. I did it on purpose, to prove the choice was mine."

I hadn't known this about Gwen. She'd seemed so shy and retiring by the time I knew her. That is, before she'd made her way out of Mormonism and into the police academy.

"Then I made sure he heard about it. He tried to punish me for it, but he couldn't let anyone else know what was going on, of course, because it would have ruined his reputation as the perfect father. And it might have led to someone figuring out what was really wrong," Gwen added.

"I'm so sorry," I said. And I didn't just mean it for Gwen. I meant it for Sabrina, too. I was sorry we lived in a world where Kurt and I at our absolute worst were still the best kind of family that Sabrina could imagine.

"Make sure she knows you're rock solid. That nothing she does will make you think it's her fault. Got it?" Gwen asked fiercely. "And I'll think about it over the next few days. I've had training on this in my classes, but it's different in real life."

"Thank you," I said. "I really appreciate it."

"No, thank you," Gwen said. "For her sake, and for mine."

I wiped my tears away as she hung up. At least Gwen had survived everything that had happened to her, and now she could understand someone like Sabrina. It was a terrible connection to be relieved about, but somehow I was. I couldn't thank God about it, though. Sometimes I just couldn't go that far.

CHAPTER 20

The next morning, Kurt woke me up with a kiss. "You remember the ward Christmas party is tonight?" he said.

"I remember," I muttered. I had signed up to bring five dozen homemade rolls, and normally, I'd be happy to spend the day baking. But with Sabrina here, I wasn't sure that was the best use of my time.

"I could get store-bought ones," Kurt offered.

"No," I said, because no one deserved to eat store-bought rolls for Christmas.

It would take me most of the day to get through a triple batch of my regular recipe, which meant I couldn't entertain Sabrina. Maybe she'd think it was fun to help? Another family activity she wouldn't likely have done at home.

I poked my head into the bedroom and found that she was gone—again. And the window was still open. No wonder the whole house was so cold.

I went immediately to the bathroom, but the door was open and the lights were off. She wasn't there.

Back in Zachary's old bedroom, I looked down at the roof and the cement landing beyond it. How hard would it have been for her to climb out that way? And then what would she have done? My car was still in the driveway. We lived so far up the mountain in Draper that it would take her hours to walk down to the FrontRunner station or any stores. And was she planning to leave everything from our shopping trip here?

I closed the window, then went downstairs, calling for Sabrina in as level a voice I could manage despite my panic.

She was down in the basement this time, with a backpack from Zachary's room that she was filling with cans of chili, Spam, tuna fish, chicken—anything with protein.

I watched her in silence for a few seconds. She skipped canned vegetables or anything that had to be cooked, like instant ramen or mac and cheese. She also skipped anything that wasn't food, like the huge plastic containers of toilet paper, the rows of shampoo and conditioner, shaving cream, soap, and dishwashing liquid.

"Sabrina?" I said quietly.

She froze, not turning around.

"What's going on?" I asked.

She turned to face me, and I could see her mind spinning a story right there. "I thought I would take some things up into my bedroom. Then if I got hungry in the middle of the night and didn't want to come all the way downstairs, I could just eat," she said.

I appreciated her attempt to make up a believable story and decided to play along. As much as I wanted her to stay, I wouldn't try to stop her—like Gwen had told me last night, she had to feel in control.

"Do you have a can opener?" I asked her.

"What?"

"For those cans. You'll need something to open them with. Just a second." I rummaged through the camp gear in the opposite corner and came up with a tiny camp can opener. "Here. Put this in."

She looked guilty, but she took it. "Thanks," she said, head down.

"Maybe you should take some water, too," I said.

As I handed her water bottles, she accepted as many as she could fit.

"That good?" I asked.

"Yeah," she said and tried to put the backpack on. It nearly pulled her over backward. She had to hold her arms out to keep steady.

"Maybe you shouldn't load it up so much," I offered.

"No, I'm fine," she said. "Really."

"I could get you a duffle bag instead. It would hold more," I suggested. I turned away, trying not to cry. I didn't want to think about what it would be like to look in her room in the morning and find it empty.

I loved the story "The Prodigal Son," but what happened when your children didn't come back? Did you keep just waiting for the rest of your life? What if they weren't even really your children?

I had to stop thinking of me and think of Sabrina instead. She needed to feel safe. I would be damned if I wouldn't help her with that. Safety was what I was best at!

"Actually, there are a few more things here it might be good for you to have." I gestured at the full range of camping gear.

"Oh, I couldn't take that stuff," she said, backing away as I

held out the titanium spork I'd bought Samuel for his eigh-
teenth birthday. He hadn't had the chance to use it yet.

"There's a camp stove and some fuel in here. Matches.
Camp mess kit." I handed her the cup, bowl, plate, and
matching silverware. "Here are some water purification tab-
lets. Take a tent, too." She hadn't brought back her sleeping
bag with her. It had probably gone to good use by Missy or
one of the others.

She looked at the tent, then leaned forward and ran a
finger up and down it.

"Look, I've got to get started making some rolls for the
ward Christmas party tonight. Do you want to come with us,
or should I leave some dinner here for you?"

Her eyes widened. "You'd want me to come?" she asked.

"Of course. We'll just say you're my niece who's visiting
from out of town," I said with a wink.

She laughed. "Okay. It could be fun, right?"

Relief washed over me. Even if she was one step out the
door, this meant another day of a roof over her head. "Fun in
a certain way," I said. "And if you're interested in keeping busy
today, you can help me with the rolls. I could use a hand in a
couple of hours when I have dough for shaping."

I saw Sabrina take the backpack and a few of the camp
items to her room. It was quiet up there for a while, and I
resisted the impulse to go and check on her while the first
batch of dough was rising.

She came down right when it was ready to be shaped, and
I showed her how to make knots, spirals, and hearts.

"I like how it feels in my hands. It's so soft. Like playdough,"
Sabrina said.

"Yeah, I remember making playdough for my boys when they were little. We used food coloring and sometimes glitter to smoosh in it." The glitter had usually gotten into more than the playdough.

Sabrina stared at me. "You made your own playdough, too?" she asked.

I laughed. "It's easy," I said. "Just flour and water and salt cooked over the stove in a pot."

"I want to be like you when I grow up," she said earnestly. Then she looked down at her hands. "Well, not that I could be."

"Of course you can. You can be anything you want after you graduate from high school and go to college. Have you thought about that?" I hoped this wouldn't pressure or offend her.

"Yeah," she said. "I have." Her tone wasn't very optimistic.

"Kurt is an accountant," I blathered on. "When the boys were younger, they all wanted to be just like him. By the time they were in high school, though, they all thought it was the most boring job ever. So we made up lists of other possibilities. Space exploration. Writing Hollywood scripts. Running for president."

Sabrina grunted. This didn't seem to cheer her up.

"You really can be anything you want," I said.

"Well, maybe some people can," Sabrina said, and I noticed then that she'd been playing with that ball of dough for so long, it had turned gray and lifeless.

I took it and gave her a new one. But I stopped with the questions about her future, and we chatted instead about SpongeBob and other harmless topics.

CHAPTER 21

When Kurt got home from work and immediately headed upstairs to get dressed, I joined him, changing out of my flour-dusted clothes and into a red, velvety Christmas dress that I'd probably worn every year since I'd bought it. Kurt was taking off his suit for what might be the first time this year as bishop and into a holiday sweater the boys had bought him years ago—one with all twelve reindeer on it, including Rudolph, front and center with his big red nose. Once upon a time, it had had little bells all over it, but those had fallen off, thank God. And if I'd helped them a bit one day in the laundry room, that information would be staying with me.

"Is Sabrina coming?" he asked.

"She said she was. We're going to say she's our niece."

"I'm sorry?" he said, running fingers through his hair, or what was left of it.

"Our niece. I'm going to tell people she's our niece," I said.

Kurt turned around to face me. "You're going to lie to the members of our ward?"

"What do you think we should say?" I asked.

He paused, then shrugged. "Why do we have to say any-thing? It's no one else's business."

I rolled my eyes at that. How could Kurt be bishop of this ward and still not understand something as basic as gossip?

When it was time, I went upstairs and knocked on Sabrina's door and asked if she was ready to go.

"Come in," she said.

I walked in to find her dressed in jeans and one of the new sweaters I'd bought her at the mall. "We'll be ready in just a few minutes. You're not going to change your mind and want to come back here, are you? Should I give you a spare key?"

"I don't think you need to do that. I'll be fine." She smiled shyly.

Within a few minutes, we were driving to the party with Sabrina in the back, along with five dozen homemade rolls that smelled, if I did say so myself, rather scrumptious.

Sabrina said, "I used to ask my parents to take me to see Santa every year. They never got around to it, and now I'm too old for that kind of stuff."

"You're never too old for Santa," Kurt said.

Sabrina snorted at that.

"The real magic happens when you're a parent yourself. Then you get to play Santa and all the elves," I said, thinking back to some very good days when the boys were young—and some very bad photos.

Sabrina's eyebrows rose. "Actually, I think of you more as Mrs. Claus." She laughed.

She sounded so normal. Happy, even. I hoped tonight would stave off her desire to leave.

When we walked in the back door near the kitchen, I stopped and took a good sniff. The building smelled like every kind of gingerbread and chocolate you could imagine, all blended together into one delicious cake with whipped cream on top.

There was also a lot of noise. Little children in nativity costumes were running around everywhere in the halls: sheep, wise men carrying packages and nearly falling over in their bathrobes, angels with tinsel haloes, shepherds with staffs and bath towels around their heads. I could hear a piano being banged through "When Joseph Went to Bethlehem," a uniquely Mormon Christmas song about how seriously and reverently Joseph took his role of fatherhood of the Christ child.

I made my way to the cultural hall, where a long table had been set up, and placed two trays of fresh rolls there, then motioned to Kurt and Sabrina to put down theirs. After that, Kurt was waylaid by the Primary President, who wanted him to read the narrator's part for the program. I pulled Sabrina to the side, but we were soon surrounded by ward members, including Anna Torstensen, who were eager to meet and welcome Sabrina.

"This is my dear friend, Anna," I said, realizing I hadn't talked to Anna for at least a month. We used to go on a walk two or three times a week. And then we just . . . stopped. I still didn't know if we were ever going to start up again. "Anna, this is my niece, Sabrina."

"Nice to meet you, Sabrina," Anna said. But she looked suspicious. She knew me well enough that I would've mentioned a close niece by now.

"She's staying with us for a little while."

"In the middle of the school year?" Anna asked.

Sabrina tensed, and I made my choice. "Yes," I said simply. Sabrina's safety took precedence over Anna's curiosity. I'd catch up Anna on this later. When things had settled down and I wasn't so afraid of Sabrina bolting every second.

I continued to introduce Sabrina around. Kurt was playing bishop, but I was the bishop's wife, and that meant everyone wanted to talk to me. They were also clearly curious about Sabrina.

Dinner was real ham crusted with ginger cookies and mustard around the bone, cheesy potato casseroles (my recipe), rolls, and green beans that Anna and a couple other women in the ward had canned by hand. Dessert was Jell-O salad, substandard in my opinion. But, clearly, no one had asked me, or I'd have volunteered to bring two dozen pies, too.

Sabrina enjoyed the food and seemed to be comfortable enough in the company. The program was coming next, and I asked her if she wanted to come to the restroom with me. She said no, so I went on my own.

I'd seen stares at Sabrina and had assumed there were some whispers but didn't realize how bad it was until I was coming out of the women's restroom near the end of the party and overheard two men talking by the drinking fountain next to the kitchen.

"Maybe she's one of his sons' castoffs," said one of my son's former Young Men's leaders, who should have known by now that Samuel had come out. "If she's pregnant, they might let her stay with them until the baby's born and she gives it up for adoption."

"You mean Samuel? If he's on a mission, he should be sent home, shouldn't he?" said one of the former counselors, who also should have known better.

"I guess a bishop can bend the rules if it's for his own son." I wanted to laugh. The thought that Kurt would break the rules for his own sons—it was not only offensive but plainly untrue. Kurt was *not* a rule breaker under any circumstances. Not to mention that Samuel wouldn't have had any interest in . . . well, it was all so ridiculous and stereotypical at the same time.

I waited until I heard them walk away because I didn't trust myself to stay calm in a confrontation. Then I noticed that Sabrina had come out of the kitchen as I'd headed back in. I suspected she'd also overheard their conversation. Her face was a little red, but she didn't say anything.

"How's it going?" I asked.

"Fine," she said. "Typical ward Christmas party." Was it just me, or was that a biting undertone?

I thought about how unfair it was that she was here in exile from her own ward because of someone else's actions. Mormonism had so many good sides. And just when I'd accepted that, I was reminded of the bad sides, too.

I put an arm around her shoulder in an attempt to comfort her. She started, nearly jumping away from me.

"I'm sorry," I said. "I didn't mean to frighten you."

She smoothed down her sweater and looked away. "No, it's my fault. I shouldn't react like that. I just—I'm not ready for anyone to touch me."

I remembered what Gwen had said about her needing to be in control of everything, and of course, this extended to her own body. I should have realized she would still be sensitive to touch.

"No one here will hurt you," I said. "You know that, right?"

She let out a harsh laugh. "You mean, except the people who think I'm worth nothing?" She made a gesture to where the two men we'd just overheard had been.

I could feel her sharp pain of being berated again and again, even here, miles away, where no one knew her. "I'm sorry," I said, because they were never going to say it, even though she was owed those words and so much more.

"My mom would say it's because I'm dressed wrong," Sabrina said, looking down at herself.

There was nothing wrong with what she was wearing. A long-sleeved sweater and jeans was the most innocuous outfit in the world. But that wasn't the point.

"It's not your problem. It's theirs," I said.

"She'd say the sweater is too tight, and so are the jeans, or that I looked at them wrong or said the wrong thing. Or smelled too sexy. Or something. It's always about me. Always my fault."

I stood there, waiting for more, though keenly aware that in the hallway next to the kitchen during a Christmas social was possibly the worst time and place to have a very private conversation.

"Sometimes I think it would be nice if I had that much power. Then I wouldn't have to—" She stopped speaking abruptly and put a hand to her mouth like this might throw up, but she didn't.

"Maybe we should go home," I said.

"But what about your husband?" she asked.

"He can walk," I said. Or, more likely, someone would offer him a ride because he was the bishop.

I walked Sabrina to the unlocked truck, then went back in to get the keys from Kurt and explain to him that we were leaving. It was right in the middle of the nativity, when the angels were singing. I was sure everyone was staring daggers at me for interrupting. But Sabrina was more important than this tradition.

As I walked toward the truck, I couldn't see Sabrina's silhouette inside, and for a moment, I thought she had gone. But when I opened the door, I saw she was just slumped in the passenger seat. She sat up when I stepped in, and we drove home in silence.

"I have a friend," I said.

"That Anna whatever-her-name-was?" Sabrina asked, rolling her eyes.

"No, not Anna. Her name is Gwen. She's not in this ward anymore. She's in training to be a police officer."

"Police?" Sabrina said. It was clear the thought alone made her anxious.

"In training," I corrected. "She was abused by her father when she was younger. She went back to the police academy because she wanted to be able to help other people who were victimized like she was. She wanted to make the system better."

"Well, good for her." Sabrina sounded bitter. No, more just exhausted.

"I talked to her about you last night."

"What?" She frowned at me. "Why would you do that?"

"No personal details, I promise." I shouldn't have said

anything, I knew it now. Gwen had told me to make her feel safe. "I wanted some advice on how to help, that's all." I sighed.

"You've already helped me plenty," Sabrina said.

I wasn't sure that sounded like a compliment. How had things gone so badly since our board game night on Monday? Because I had a unique capacity to say too much.

"If you want to talk to her, I could give you her number. We could also try a therapist," I said, pulling into the driveway.

Sabrina stiffened as I tried to touch her shoulder again.

"I'm sorry. I shouldn't have—"

"I don't need to talk to a therapist. I'm not crazy," Sabrina said.

"Of course you're not," I said. And then I really did stop talking because I was only likely to make it worse.

Sabrina went to bed as soon as we got home, and so did I. Kurt woke me when he came in. Then I couldn't fall back asleep, sure every sound I heard was Sabrina leaving. But in the morning, she was still there.

CHAPTER 22

Kurt went off to work the next morning, and I wrote what might be my last email of the year to Samuel on his mission. Then I got to work on cleaning the house for Christmas.

"Can I talk to you?" asked Sabrina a couple of hours later as I scrubbed the toilet in her bathroom.

"Of course," I said. I washed my hands and walked downstairs with her so we could sit on the living room couches.

"What's up?" I was hoping that she was going to open up to me more about what had happened to her—maybe even ask for some therapy? It was probably too much to think she was ready to talk to the police.

"Well, it's—" she started.

Then the doorbell rang, and I excused myself briefly, leaving my phone behind. When I got to the porch, the Ringels' youngest daughter, Emma, was holding out a plate of Christmas goodies wrapped in a festive snowflake bag and a gift tag on the porch.

"Oh, thank you. This looks lovely," I said. Inside the bag were chocolate-covered cinnamon bears, probably hand-dipped, with red and green sprinkles on top.

"Merry Christmas!" Emma said. Four years ago, I'd been her Sunday School teacher. I remembered her as an awkward but earnest early preteen. She was taller now, though still shy, and must have been a sophomore or junior in high school.

"Are you having fun on your Christmas break?" I asked.

"Yeah, mostly because I don't have any homework," she said, glancing back at the car, where her parents were waiting for her.

"Oh, I'm sure you have quite a few more plates to deliver."

"I miss you teaching my Sunday School class, you know," she said.

"Oh, that's very kind of you."

"Even though my parents thought you were saying dangerous things, it was a relief to be able to actually ask real questions out loud," she said, then hurried off.

I paused before waving goodbye to the Ringels. I hadn't thought I'd been so radical four years ago, but I guess I had. Interesting to know what other people had thought.

I brought the goodies inside, and that was when I noticed that my phone was in a different spot from where I left it. At least, I was pretty sure it was. I thought back to a moment before and realized the phone might have been unlocked because I'd been looking up a recipe.

Had Sabrina been poking around in it? Why would she do that?

It made no sense, I told myself, so I held out the plate of chocolate-covered cinnamon bears and offered them to Sabrina.

"Thanks," she said, her tone distant. She popped one into her mouth.

"You said you wanted to talk to me about something?"

She didn't look at me. "Yeah. Well, I just wanted to say I really appreciate what you and your husband are doing for me. Thank you so much."

"You're welcome," I said. Should I say anything about the recording? Had she listened to it? Surely she hadn't had the time for that. But she could have sent it to herself fairly quickly, then deleted the outgoing message. "You don't have to keep thanking us, you know. We're helping you because we care about you. We want you to feel safe here."

I put the phone into my pocket, wishing that I'd taken it with me when I stepped outside. Or sent the recording to the police already. Then it would be out of my hands. But what must it look like that it was still on my phone? I hadn't even listened to it myself yet.

"I want to get you and Kurt something for Christmas," Sabrina said brightly.

"Oh, you don't have to do that," I said. I wanted so much to believe that she hadn't done anything that I just let myself believe it.

"I know, but I want to," she said, smiling.

"I guess I could take you out shopping again, but it will be terrible this close to Christmas. Too many people crammed in every store."

"But I don't want you giving me money. I want to earn it. I want to give back to you." Her face was flushed.

I stood up to get my purse. I remembered my sons each asking something similar at about her age, when they were too old for an allowance and too young to get a job on their own.

Sabrina said, "My dad used to have me do lights with him.

If you want, I can put some up for you guys, too. I noticed you didn't have any, and they're nice up even after Christmas. New Year's and stuff."

Kurt hadn't done decorative Christmas lights in years, but I didn't think he had anything against them. They were usually just too much work. I wasn't sure we had any functioning ones left in the basement, though, which meant possibly spending more on lights than on labor.

Sabrina went on, "Or I could do something else. Like, um, organize your basement. Or help clean the house. All the driveways on the block seem shoveled, but if you have something else in mind, I could do that."

I thought about the long list of household things that Kurt had let go over his last two years as bishop. Samuel had tried to keep them up while he was still home, but Sabrina was right, a hand around the house would be helpful.

"Lights sound good," I said. "And the help you've already given me in the kitchen counts, too."

"You're going to pay me to help make the food I mostly ate myself? I don't think so," Sabrina said, her mouth twisting a bit so her crooked tooth poked into her lip.

I liked that thoughtful twisted-mouth expression. For the first time, I had a glimpse of who she might be in the future. She was already kind, thoughtful, and willing to work, even in the wake of something so traumatizing.

"You're a tough cookie, you know that?" I said.

A flicker of darkness passed over her face, then slowly faded. "I guess so," she said.

She was going to get through this. Kurt and I would help. Maybe she'd go to the police eventually and maybe she wouldn't; maybe she'd talk to Gwen and maybe she wouldn't. But she was a good kid. I was glad she was here. That she had come to stay with us, even under these circumstances. I felt this fierce happiness, and I let it grow without questioning why I needed it so much.

We drove to the local Walmart, where Sabrina had asked to go. "My dad's always telling people that if they spend money, they should spend it on help getting the lights up, not on more expensive lights. He says you should just throw them out each year because it costs more in time to replace bulbs than just buying new ones."

I stopped in the parking lot. "Isn't that bad for the environment?" I asked.

"He doesn't care about that," she said dismissively.

"Well, he might not care, but there must be some kind of restrictions in place."

"In Utah?" she scoffed. "Whatever. Recycle if you want. I'm not sure I believe there'll be much left of the planet by the time we take the problem seriously."

Such a jaded view of the world. "Do you really think that?" I asked as I got out of the car.

"Think what?" As if she'd already moved on to something else more important.

"That it's too late for the planet."

"In, like, twenty years?" A shrug. "Probably. So carpe diem and all that. You have to live in the moment."

"That seems a little dark. At your age, you should be looking forward to the future."

She shrugged. "Parts of it, sure, I guess. But my future won't be like yours. I'm not like you. I don't want the things you want."

I laughed at that. "Well, you don't have to make rolls and candy if you don't want."

"Yeah, too bad for the world, right? Less homemade candy for them."

"You have talents of your own." Surely she had to see that.

"Like what?" Sabrina asked, her head turning sharply toward me.

To be honest, I had no idea what her talents were. It hit me then that I didn't know her very well at all, despite that moment of connection a few minutes ago. But I said, "Like strategy. I saw you in that game with Kurt. You're brilliant and ruthless. The business world could use someone like you. Or politics. You could be president someday."

She thought this over for a moment. Then she nodded. "Brilliant and ruthless. I'll take that," she said.

It seemed like enough.

We headed into the Walmart and shouted over other shoppers and über-cheery Christmas music, filled a huge cart with lights—all white, Sabrina insisted, having learned this from her father. They cost six hundred dollars, which I hoped Kurt wouldn't notice amidst all the other Christmas bills.

"You're sure we need all of this?" I asked.

"I'm sure," she said confidently. "You always want too many lights instead of too few. We can take the extras back for a refund if I don't use them all. But if you're going to do lights, you might as well do them right." She sounded so invested that I didn't argue with her.

"I don't want to make the neighbors feel like they have to outdo us or anything," I said, smiling. Plenty of people did lights, but it was usually a single strand across the roof and maybe a couple of trees in the front yard. We didn't have anyone in the ward who went whole hog or paid for lights to be put up. Would this make it look like the bishop thought he was more important than others in the ward?

"It's going to be great," Sabrina said as we checked out. She helped me with the miles-long receipt and made sure to put the card back in my purse. "You have a ladder at home, right?"

"Yes, we do. Somewhere in the garage." I was becoming more and more nervous about this. I wasn't her real mother, and I didn't know if this was safe. What if something happened to her?

CHAPTER 23

It was nearly dark by the time we got home, so Sabrina said she'd put up the lights the next day. I made some fettucine alfredo with shrimp for dinner. Not something most people thought of as a holiday meal, but it was simple and rich and satisfying, so I always made it at least once around Christmas.

One year, Samuel complained because I'd served it three times in a week. That was the year I was in the Primary Presidency and had used up most of my mental energy on the nativity play for the ward Christmas party, for which I was a de facto director.

Kurt came home and ate. He chatted with Sabrina. "There's a service project coming up after Christmas. The youth are going to make some hygiene kits for the homeless."

I thought this was a little too on the nose.

Sabrina bristled. "You really think that helps homeless people? Giving them shampoo and soap?"

"Well, what do you think would help them?" Kurt asked. "Food?"

"Money," Sabrina said bluntly.

"Well . . ." Kurt hesitated.

"You don't trust them. You think they'd buy drugs with it or something like that. So you buy them soap instead. Really helpful. Clean a man for a day, and then he won't stink all year, right?" Her sarcasm was thick.

I winced, but I didn't try to defend Kurt. He had stepped right into this.

"You were there. You must have seen plenty of drug use. Do you think that helps people get back on track with their lives?" Kurt asked.

"Back on track," Sabrina sneered. "What you mean is that you'll only give them help as long as they're working to get your gold star."

Kurt put up his hands. "Look, I said we were trying to help. But I also don't want the youth in our ward to do anything dangerous. Hygiene kits are a good compromise."

"Dangerous?" Sabrina echoed. "Sure, protect the kids in your ward. The good Mormon boys and girls who pretend they're following your rules, which makes them deserving of your protection, unlike the homeless."

Sabrina was breathing hard, and I think Kurt realized that he'd unintentionally touched on something more deep-seated.

"I'm not defending anyone. Criminals don't get a pass because they're Mormon," he said.

"Don't they?" Sabrina asked.

Kurt's expression darkened. "You say the word, and I'll call the police here right now. You can give them a statement, and I'll make sure you have the best therapist money can buy. I can't control the legal system, but if there's a civil case to be made, I'll pay for a lawyer, too. But you have to face up to what happened to you instead of trying to run away from it, Sabrina," he said.

He glanced over at me, as if expecting me to agree with him. But I was speechless. Kurt always meant well, but sometimes he really was a bull in a china shop.

"Always on your terms. Well, no thanks." Sabrina stomped back up the stairs and slammed the door to her room.

"She has to go to the police if she wants justice," he said, turning toward me. "Or, at least, she has to start confronting what happened to her. We can't keep dancing around the subject."

I sighed. "I know. It's going to take a while for her to trust us, I think."

"We don't have a while, Linda," he said. "She's not staying here forever." Then he went into his office and I went to bed.

ON FRIDAY MORNING, I looked out the window as I started to make some oatmeal for breakfast and saw it was snowing. Sabrina came tramping downstairs a few minutes later in full winter gear and work boots she must have found in Zachary's closet because they were too big for her.

I didn't comment. I wanted to offer up my own boots but was pretty sure she wouldn't accept. "Eat some breakfast before you head out," I said. "Maybe it will stop snowing."

I'd checked the forecast, though, and it didn't look likely.

She ate her oatmeal dutifully, though it clearly wasn't her favorite. Kurt had never liked it, either, but I forced it on him because it was good for him.

When Sabrina had rinsed her dish and put it in the dishwasher, she looked out the window again. "I'm sure I'll be fine," she said. "I'm tough."

I didn't doubt that, but she'd said it as if she needed to prove it to herself.

"Please be safe. I don't want you in the hospital for the holidays on my conscience." I made a wide-eyed face to show I was joking.

"I'll be fine. I've done this a million times before," she said.

"Maybe I could pay you in advance for the work on the lights and you can go get any last presents today while it's snowing. Then you can do the lights tomorrow, when it's supposed to be clear. What do you think?" I thought she would refuse, but she paused, then nodded with a sigh.

"All right. Just this once," she said. "Because Christmas is coming up so fast, and it'll take longer to put these up while it's snowing."

"Well, if I'm going to pay you in advance, how many hours do you think it'll take?" We'd always paid the kids double minimum wage for work around the house because we wanted them to feel appreciated—and also because we made the boys save half their money for a mission. But there was no mission fund required here.

"If I work all day Saturday and Sunday, that would be twenty hours, I think," she said after a moment's calculation. "I figure that's worth about four hundred dollars. Then I can get you and Kurt something really nice."

I tried not to choke at her quick estimate. Four hundred dollars was a lot more than we'd ever paid the boys at once, even knowing half was going to a future mission.

But Sabrina must have caught my expression because she immediately said, "Oh, is that too much? I probably shouldn't expect you to pay me what my father did."

Had her father really paid her twenty dollars an hour? "No, it's fine," I said after a beat. "It seems like a fair price to me. I just don't have enough cash on hand."

"We could stop at the bank on the way," Sabrina said. "Or you could give me one of your cards that isn't signed."

I didn't have any credit cards that weren't signed, and I wouldn't give one to anyone if I did. It wasn't just the risk of loss—on the outside chance of anyone asking her for ID, I didn't want her getting in trouble.

"I'll get you some cash out of the ATM on our way," I said, sending Kurt a text.

Dropping Sabrina off at the mall. Paid her ahead of time for the lights so she can buy presents. Love you.

We headed to the bank, and I withdrew the four hundred, handing it to her.

She folded it and put it into her coat pocket immediately. At least she knew not to flash money in public.

Then I dropped her off at the South Towne mall and told her to text me that she was ready to be picked up. I felt a pang, remembering how often I'd done this with one or more of my sons. But never a daughter.

But no, Sabrina wasn't Georgia. I didn't think of her that way, no matter what Kurt said.

As I drove off, I was a little worried she might not come back. I'd just handed her four hundred dollars in cash and dropped her very close to a Blue Line train station. She could easily take TRAX back to downtown Salt Lake City and rejoin

Missy and the others. But did I really think she would do that? Even from a practical standpoint, she had a backpack full of rations at our house that she'd be leaving behind.

I drove home and read Anne Perry's new novel, getting lost in late Victorian London for a few hours. I was surprised at how much time had passed when my phone chirped at me. But I was enormously relieved. Sabrina was ready for me to pick her up. I drove to the north mall entrance and got out to help her carry things in, but she had only two small bags on her arm.

She smiled at my shock and said, "Good things come in small packages, Mrs. Wallheim," followed by the most radiant smile I'd ever seen on her. It transformed her completely, and four hundred dollars was a bargain to see that kind of joy.

"You should really call me Linda," I said.

"I don't know," she said, as she climbed in. "It feels weird."

"How about Sister Wallheim, then?" After the words came out, I cursed myself, realizing it might remind her of her ward and what had happened there.

"I can do Sister Wallheim if you want," she said anyway.

We drove home, and she offered to help me with dinner.

"I checked the forecast, and it looks like tomorrow will be cold and clear," she said.

"The real question is whether the snow will ice over," I said. It was light enough now that it was easier to drive than it had been when I'd dropped her off, which I was grateful for.

In the kitchen, I set her to work on a salad and I made some clam chowder, an old recipe of my mother's. She and I had had some problems, but she had taught me to cook, and this was a recipe I cherished. I told Sabrina about it as I went.

"I don't offer this recipe to very many people." In fact, I

had never given it to anyone else. Somehow, it had never felt right to pass it to one of my daughters-in-law. "I could give it to you."

"Oh, wow. Thanks!" she said. She seemed pleased, though as soon as I had written it down and offered it to her on a notecard, I wondered whether she would ever actually use it. But then she took a picture of it on her phone, and I decided that if she was going to that much trouble, she must have wanted it after all. She kept tasting it as it bubbled on the stove, and by the time Kurt got home, she must have had at least a bowl of it in spoonfuls.

I hadn't had time to make a full batch of rolls, but I had made buttermilk biscuits from scratch. I kept buttermilk in the fridge purely for cooking. I thought it was nasty for drinking, but the biscuits it made were fluffy and buttery. We all had mouths too full to talk until dinner was over.

Kurt excused himself to go to bed early, and I didn't blame him. Sabrina said she wanted to get a head start on the lights in the morning.

So it was just me and my Anne Perry book for the night.

CHAPTER 24

I n the morning, I heard Sabrina outside with the ladder just
before light and went out in my pajamas with my coat over
them to ask her if she needed breakfast.

"I'll take a break in a few hours when I'm cold," she said.

"What's your favorite hot breakfast?" I asked her. "So I can
have it ready when you're done."

She told me pancakes and sausages. I asked her if we could
do bacon instead, since I didn't have sausages on hand, and
got no answer—she must not have heard me. But I was afraid
of shouting in case the distraction made her shaky on the
ladder.

To my everlasting regret, I went back inside and heard a
terrible thump and crack about twenty minutes later. I immediately rushed out and saw the first row of lights dangling
above our front porch and Sabrina on her back in the snow.

"Are you all right?" I asked, my heart thumping with terror.

She managed to laugh, though there was a groan of pain
underneath it. It reassured me nonetheless that she wasn't
fatally injured. "I'm fine," she said. "I just decided to rest for
a minute before getting up again."

I bent down to offer her my arm, but she didn't take it just yet.

"I think something's wrong with my ankle," she said, pulling her foot to her chest. "It feels like it's on fire."

"We should go to the doctor," I said. It was exactly what I'd wanted to avoid because of the insurance issues and law enforcement. If her parents were called and figured out I had lied to Clint, that would be a huge mess as well.

"No," she said immediately. "I'm okay. Just maybe help me get inside and then I can rest it? If I put ice on it, it will probably be fine."

I wasn't going to agree to that until I took a look at her ankle, but getting her inside first would be difficult. I ended up waking up Kurt to help me get her onto the couch by the kitchen with a two-man lift. I'd already started making pancakes, so I kept going and brought her a stack on a plate. Her face looked pale and pinched, so I asked if she needed painkillers.

"I'm fine," she said again.

"Can I see your ankle?" I asked.

She pushed off the blanket she'd been under and tried to pull off her boot. Why hadn't she taken that off an hour ago? I should've spotted it.

I tugged at the once too-big boot and finally got it off. Underneath was an already swelling ankle. It could easily get worse, but it didn't look broken. I breathed a sigh of relief. Maybe it would be okay after all for her to just rest.

"I'll get you some ice," I said and brought that along with a glass of water and some Advil. I took away the half-eaten plate of pancakes.

Kurt glanced over at Sabrina. "Do you think that was an accident or on purpose?" he asked, quietly enough only I could hear.

What was he implying? "Go look at her ankle. Why would she do that to herself on purpose?" I said just as quietly.

He hesitated, poking at his stack of pancakes. "Linda, have you considered that she's playing you?" he asked.

"What? She's a teenager. She's not playing anything," I insisted.

"Didn't you just give her several hundred dollars?" he asked.

"She spent it on presents. For us," I scolded. How dared he imply she was being selfish?

"Hmm," Kurt said. "Did you see what she bought?"

"No, but they're surprises." I hated that I was starting to feel suspicious, tempted now to go sneak upstairs and check her bags.

"All right, well, I've got to talk to the Amoses. Hopefully I'll have time to head over to work for a few hours after that. I've got a bunch of business emergencies there that I haven't had time to deal with." He gave me a perfunctory kiss and went on his way.

I took care of Sabrina all day, bringing her food and drink. But despite my wanting to give her the benefit of the doubt, I did go outside once to look at the ladder's position on the sidewalk. Kurt had really made me regret advancing her that money. But at some point, I just had to trust Sabrina, like I wanted her to trust me.

THAT NIGHT, I went up to say goodnight. She gave me a big hug and thanked me for helping her all day. Her ankle seemed to be hurting her less now, and she'd even made a couple of trips up and down the stairs throughout the evening.

"Sister Wallheim, you really are the nicest person I've ever met," she said. "I'm so glad you came into my life."

I felt exactly the same.

As I released her small, thin frame from the hug, Sabrina wiped at her cheek self-consciously. "Sorry, I didn't mean to be so mushy."

"It's been so nice having you around," I said, despite my determination to coax her back to her parents after Christmas.

And I knew that, eventually, she would have to leave—because she needed to, even if I would be alone again.

CHAPTER 25

Sunday morning on Christmas Eve, I woke up and rushed around, preparing pumpkin pecan waffles with a sweet cinnamon orange juice syrup. Sabrina was already up and dressed. I told her she didn't have to worry about doing the lights with her ankle injury, but she insisted and walked around a bit to show me she was fine. I told her to come back inside immediately if she felt any pain and to keep her phone on her in case something happened again.

Kurt and I drove to church together with the heat on high. He'd canceled everything but sacrament meeting and for once didn't have to be there early as bishop. It was a lovely service, with Christmas songs and talks about the grace of Jesus, which was something I'd been wanting to hear for ages instead of lessons on sleeve lengths, not criticizing the leaders of the church, cleaning the church building next week, and going to the temple. Everyone seemed to be in a good mood and happy to see me. It was only an hour long, too, so no time to argue doctrinal points.

I felt so good that I waited around for twenty minutes after the service was over for Kurt to drive home with me. He didn't have his usual responsibilities because of Christmas, and I snuggled up next to him in the cab on the way home. Everything was going so well, like I'd fallen back into the best parts of my old life. Maybe I could let go of some of my complaining about the church and look for the good instead. Maybe things were okay after all.

When we got to our house, I didn't realize anything was wrong for several minutes, only that the front door hadn't been closed all the way. Had that been me? Or had Sabrina gone out and not closed it properly behind her?

I went up to her room, but she wasn't there. For just a moment, I told myself she was just out on a walk.

But then I saw the backpack and all the shopping bags were gone.

I backed out of the room and heard Kurt calling to me, but I couldn't parse what he was saying.

"Linda? Linda, can you hear me?" Kurt was standing in front of me.

I nodded and sagged into him, sobbing. "She's gone."

He tugged, trying to get me to sit down on Zachary's bed, but I couldn't. It was where Sabrina belonged.

I stumbled downstairs to the kitchen. Kurt got me some of my holiday herbal tea, gingerbread. I don't remember if he put any sugar or milk in it. It hardly mattered. Tea was normal. Tea was comfort.

I sat at the bar, hunched over it. I thought about last night, when she'd told me she was glad we met. It seemed that had been her goodbye.

I made my way the front room, where the Christmas tree remained, the presents still beneath—including Sabrina's.

The lights winked at me, and the ornaments clinked cheerily as if they didn't notice anything wrong.

Whatever it was Sabrina had bought on her last shopping trip, she'd taken it with her. And she'd chosen the one hour she knew we'd be gone, while we were at church. No wonder Sabrina had insisted I didn't have to stay.

I thought about all the time she'd spent on her phone since she'd been here. It had never occurred to me to wonder who she had been in contact with. It had never occurred to me that when Missy had nudged Sabrina to come with me at the convenience store, they might have been planning this all along. I'd been so naïve.

Then I saw the note taped up to the back of the garage door. Sabrina must have put it there so I'd only see it when I knew she was gone, when it was too late to stop her.

Mrs. Wallheim,

I wanted to thank you for your help and say I'm sorry I left like this. I know you would have wanted to say goodbye, but I didn't want to try to explain why I had to go. You've been so kind, and it's not your fault I left. You didn't do anything wrong.

I don't want you to blame yourself for anything that happens after this, either. All of it was planned out before you came and found me. There was no way you could have changed my mind. The police don't do anything for girls like me. It would have just been more shaming and mocking but in front of cameras. What

happened to me was the kind of thing that you can't
get justice for through the system. Not real justice.
   I think if things had been different, if I had been dif-
ferent, it would have been nice to stay with a family
like yours. But I have to do this my way.

Sabrina

I was weeping long before I got to the end of the letter, but I wouldn't let Kurt see it until I'd finished reading it.

"What do you think she's going to do?" I asked him, shaking as I thought over the possibilities.

"I don't know. Nothing good." His lips were pressed together grimly.

"Can we call the police and, I don't know, warn them?"

Kurt gave me a long, sad look. "We should have called them days ago, Linda. We should have had her go in and make a statement. Now that she's gone, what can we do? It's not illegal for her to be on the streets, and it's not like we can warn them about some vague plan."

But he reread the letter, and so did I.

"What if she's going to do something to Jonathan and Peyton?" I asked, remembering the way she'd argued with Kurt when he'd tried to convince her to go to the police.

"What are the police going to do on Christmas Eve? Send a patrol to their houses to check that they're safe?" Kurt asked. "There aren't enough of them here to yank them from home for that."

"What if we call their families and warn them to stay safe?" I asked.

"Is that what you want to do?" Kurt asked me firmly. "Because I'll do it if you insist, but I really don't know whose side we're on at this point. If we call and Sabrina and her friends get caught trying to vandalize their homes or something, they could all end up in jail. If anyone is of legal age, they could go to prison."

This was the Kurt I had always loved, not the Kurt in the therapist's office. When things got bad, Kurt became his best self. I let go of a breath. I was okay here. He knew what to do. Listen to him.

I finally asked him to text Joseph and tell him that Sabrina had run away and might have some kind of revenge plan.

"All right, I've texted him, but I'm not sure what he can do, either. It's not his job to protect those boys, you know. He's only their Sunday School teacher." He tried to pat my shoulder, but I pulled away.

I read the note a few more times until I basically had it memorized.

Kurt tried to turn on the TV, but it was no more than background noise. Somehow, it was dark again, and I realized I should have been thinking about dinner. We hadn't had anything since breakfast. Time had seemed to slow to complete stillness, then slip away from me entirely.

"I'll call for a pizza," Kurt said.

I didn't argue with him, though we would normally never do that on a Sunday.

"I thought I was keeping her safe," I got out, my voice not sounding like my own. It was too flat and shaky and high-pitched.

"She's a victim, Linda. And probably still hurting. But I

think you should let her go. This is the end of it for us. All right?"

I nodded sadly. What more could I do?

"Someone must have picked her up," I said, thinking through the timing of all this. Who had a car? Missy? Jonathan? Peyton?

"It's not your problem anymore, Linda," Kurt said.

I leaned into him, too despondent to even cry again.

Kurt kissed me gently on the top of the head. "You should head to bed."

On another day, maybe I would have been mad that he was telling me what to do. I'd have called it patriarchy, but I was too tired to do that, so I followed him upstairs.

Kurt tucked me in, pulling the blanket up to my chin. "Remember, we get our phone call with Samuel tomorrow. A whole hour to talk with him."

I tried to think about what hopeful thing I could possibly say to Samuel after all this. *This is how people are. This is why they're worth saving. Or are they?*

CHAPTER 26

I tried to go to sleep but couldn't. Tomorrow was Christmas Day. The boys and their families would be here around noon. I had a big dinner to get ready. The turkey was thawing in the fridge. And Sabrina would be back out in the cold while we were inside, enjoying an indulgent meal and the security of home and family. Whatever her plans were, she didn't deserve to be alone on Christmas.

I tossed and turned.

There had been a couple of difficult Christmas Eve nights when the boys had been small that I'd survived on almost no sleep, but that had been years ago, when my own youth had supplied me with much more energy.

I remembered one particular Christmas when we'd put the boys to bed early because we'd needed extra time to finish preparing the surprises we had planned for the next day. Samuel had been a toddler then. As we'd tried frantically to put together bicycles, the boys had come downstairs one by one and thrown up. One on the stairs, one on the kitchen floor, one in the living room right by the tree. I'd taken them all back upstairs and cleaned them up. Kurt had taken care of the floors and continued the wrapping and Christmas preparations. I'd slept on the floor in Zachary's room for a couple of hours before waking and hearing another of the boys throw up.

Christmas morning, they'd all woken up a little late but happy and healthy. It had been a twenty-four-hour flu. Or twelve hours, I supposed. We had Christmas dinner as usual, and it wasn't until night that Kurt and I succumbed to it and started vomiting ourselves. That was such a sweet memory for me now. Would Christmas ever feel the same without little kids at home?

After finishing up some work, Kurt came upstairs and climbed into bed next to me. He was cold to the touch, and I instinctively pulled away from him.

"Sorry," he muttered. He must have fallen asleep about ten seconds after that because he started snoring.

I nudged him to roll over and the snoring stopped, but I still couldn't sleep. I kept thinking about Sabrina and the hug she had given me. I kept hearing the letter she'd left, read by her shaky voice.

I got up and told myself I was just going to check the fridge for a snack and go back to bed. Sometimes it helped to give in to the insomnia for an hour or so and try again instead of just lying in bed, letting your brain sink into panic.

But I didn't check the fridge. I put on my long winter coat and hat and gloves, grabbed keys, and went out to the garage. For whatever reason, Kurt had left the garage door open when he'd come home, so I didn't even have to open it and risk waking him.

The clock in the car said that it was 3:24 A.M. I had never felt less sleepy in my life. I felt like I'd already had about six coffees as I drove down the mountainside, past the Draper temple, and onto the freeway.

If you ever want to see a deserted freeway, try driving one in Utah in the middle of the night on Christmas. I only saw about four other cars, and I easily maneuvered around them. My car had never gone so fast before. It felt as if God were putting the wind at my tail, getting me to the downtown exit in less than fourteen minutes before the day's snowfall. This time, I didn't need to find a parking spot. I didn't even drive around Pioneer Park. I went directly to the Fast Break, though I didn't see anyone out front. I parked on the street, and they came out of the convenience store as I approached: Missy, Andre, Sabrina, and the other three. Whatever Sabrina was planning, it looked like it wasn't going down yet.

My hands were shaking, but I didn't feel afraid. I was sure of myself and what I was about to do. I needed closure. To make sure this was what Sabrina wanted. Then I could let go of the fleeting moment I had thought of her as a daughter and have Christmas Day with my sons.

I locked the car with the fob and stepped out. Missy was already approaching. I turned and faced her squarely.

She stared at me, her walk slowing. I thought I read surprise in her eyes. Good.

Then I realized I hadn't even brought my purse with me. Good thing I hadn't been stopped by anyone and asked to show my license. I was still wearing my pajamas under my coat, and I felt a wave of vulnerability rise inside me.

"Linda, why are you here?" Sabrina asked in a small voice. If there had been any wind along with the snow, I wouldn't have heard her.

As it was, I locked eyes with her, and it felt for a moment as if we were the only two there. The snow was falling, but somehow I imagined we were in a snow globe, separated from the rest of the world, just her and me. Now I was Linda. "What are you planning, Sabrina?" I asked. "Trying to get vigilante revenge on those boys won't turn out well for anyone."

"She doesn't owe you anything," came Missy's harsh voice. "Not after you kept that disgusting recording. You talk about getting her justice, but you sat on proof and said nothing. You don't care about her at all."

I turned to Sabrina, agonized. "You listened to that?" I asked.

Sabrina didn't say a word, but the expression on her face said everything—she considered it a betrayal, a total breach of trust. That discovery had been the moment things had changed between us. It was when she'd asked to put up the lights for cash.

"I'm sorry I didn't tell you about it myself. I was planning to give it to the police but only if you wanted me to. They can use it against him. In a courtroom, where you can get real justice," I said, the words tumbling out of my mouth as quickly as I could form them.

Sabrina just shrugged.

I hated that shrug, a sign that she hadn't expected better of me. No one in her life had taught her that she deserved more. So of course she'd accepted what Missy was offering.

Maybe listening to the recording was the tipping point, the excuse she needed to execute their plan.

"Look, we can go to the police station right now," I said. "I can give them my phone." I patted around in my pockets but came up empty. It was probably still charging on my night-stand. Damnit!

They all raised their eyebrows at me, and I said, "We can go home and get it. I got Jonathan to make that confession because I didn't want him getting away with what he did to you."

And then I'd done nothing with it. Why?

"It doesn't matter anymore," Sabrina said, looking away.

"Of course it matters."

But she was already walking away.

"I have to do this myself, Linda," she said, turning back after a moment. "You don't know what it's like for someone to take this from you. It's like they stole me from myself. This is the only way to get it back."

I was desperate. "Please, Sabrina. Come back with me, and we'll protect you. Kurt and I will make sure the police see this through." It seemed she hadn't trusted her parents with that.

"Missy?" Sabrina said in a soft voice.

"You're going to believe her? What kind of justice does she think she's going to get for you? A slap on the wrist for those assholes? Maybe a couple weeks in a detention center? And then their lives will go on just like before. People will feel sorry for them and blame you for ruining their perfect reputations. You know they will, Sabrina," Missy said.

She sounded so cynical, and I wasn't sure she was wrong. Who was I to tell her what real life was like when I had been granted so many advantages? I'd always seen my greatest tragedy as losing Georgia, but I'd never faced anything like what Sabrina had gone through.

Sabrina's jaw tightened, her lips tightly pressed together. Her hood fell back from her head, and her hair caught the streetlight, looking almost white as it began to collect snowflakes. "Linda, you're a good person. But you and Kurt can't give me what I really need. They need to pay for what they did now, not years from now and not just with a few months in prison."

They'd taken away her self, as she'd put it. I understood her want for revenge, but why did she think prison was so easy that she'd put herself there instead of them? I wasn't going to let her do that without a fight.

"You said you felt safe," I said, "If you come back, I promise it will get better. With more time and therapy—"

Missy laughed at that, cutting me off.

I looked back at Sabrina. She had trusted me. Cared about me, at least a little. Hadn't she?

"You should go now, Linda," Sabrina said.

"I can't," I said. It was almost literal; I was shaking too much to move.

"You have a family who loves you. You shouldn't be involved in this," Sabrina said, her eyes red.

"There are so many people who love you, Sabrina," I said. "Not just me and Kurt, but Joseph and Willow and Carla. Don't you want to see her again? She's coming over today for Christmas dinner. Turkey and stuffing and all the trimmings. And my homemade pie. You've never had it, but I promise you, it's worth the trip." My smile was tremulous. Somehow I knew this wouldn't work.

"She's not going anywhere," said Missy again, this time stepping between me and Sabrina. "Sabrina, let's go get a hot chocolate. Finish up our discussion."

"Okay," Sabrina said, turning away. "I'm sorry, Linda. This is the only way I can get real justice. The only way I can be me again."

Whatever they were planning, I knew this wasn't what would make her feel whole again. That wasn't the way the world worked. Compassion was the only way to deal with real harm directed toward you without further harming yourself, and yet I also knew the thirst for someone to pay.

"Sabrina," I said, still unwilling to give up, "it's not too late. You can still change your mind."

"Go home already, Grandma," Missy said.

"Make me," I baited.

Within a fraction of a second, Missy stepped over and pushed me sharply. I fell and tasted blood as I hit the ground—had I bitten my own tongue, or was it from the asphalt?

"All I'm asking is for you to leave," Missy said, her face very close to mine, so that I could smell hints of mint on her breath, maybe from scented tobacco?

"Please, let her go," I said.

"She doesn't need you. She's with us now," Missy said.

"Did you really tell her you'd take revenge on those boys for her? Is she paying you for it?" I asked in a thread of a voice, trying to calculate how much cash she might have if she returned all the clothes I'd bought for her. Plus the lights. More than a thousand dollars, certainly.

"You better get out of here," Missy warned.

What choice did I have but to walk away? I had no concrete idea of their plan. It could involve public humiliation, a non-violent offense like vandalism, or violence. And what power did I have to stop these five teens? I wasn't with the police. I was just a middle-aged woman who wasn't sure who she was anymore.

So now I would go home and put on a good face for

Christmas dinner with my family. I'd tell myself that I'd done what I could. And I'd return to Mormonism, where women were told how much good they could do by way of the men around them. And I would feel safe there, never again at risk of experiencing this kind of hurt.

I was in the middle of the sidewalk when a car honked loudly at me. I jumped, startled, and got out of its way. Then I realized I recognized it. It was Peyton's old, beat-up pinkish-bronze Toyota. It pulled into one of the marked parking spaces, and Peyton stepped out.

I started toward him, but Missy held me back. "Don't you take this away from her," she said and waved a hand at Andre, who lumbered over and took over for her, blocking my way.

"Sabrina?" Peyton called out. "Sabrina, are you here?"

"She's in there," Missy said, waving to the convenience store.

Peyton seemed to shrug, then headed toward the front door, but by then, Sabrina was already coming out.

"Peyton, watch out!" I tried to shout.

But Andre stepped in front of me. "I don't wanna have to put a hand over your mouth, lady," he said.

I nodded, throbbing with fear. Were they planning to beat him up? Why wasn't Jonathan here, too?

"I got your message," Peyton said to Sabrina, his head low.

Andre had sagged to the side, leaning against the gas pumps, which gave me a better view. Had Sabrina called him here, or had Missy sent the text for her?

Sabrina looked just as uncomfortable as Peyton did, her shoulders high and her motions jerky.

I thought of courtroom trials. I'd been in several of them

now, and there was such care taken to make sure the accuser and the accused never had to meet like this. But maybe Sabrina could tell him directly how he had done her harm. If that was what she needed to heal and move on, then she should have it.

"Where's Jonathan?" Sabrina asked.

Peyton sighed. "It's his last Christmas with his family before his mission. He said it was important. He didn't want to come, no matter what happened if he didn't."

"He doesn't think what he did was wrong," Sabrina said. "That's what you mean. He called me a slut at school for months after what happened. He threatened me to stop me from telling anyone what he planned. Said he'd do it again."

"He says stuff like that, but I don't think he means it," Peyton tried weakly. "Look, Sabrina, he's really not a bad guy."

Not a bad guy? Were we living in the same world? How was it that this boy hadn't been raised to see that the way his friends treated other people mattered as much as the way they treated him?

"I can see him better than you can," Sabrina said. "I see you both."

Peyton looked away, then back again. "Look, I'm here because I want to make things right. Everything is just . . . so complicated. The police came and took statements from us. Did you know that?"

"And you lied," Sabrina guessed.

Peyton twitched. "Jonathan said we had to. That, otherwise, we were going to humiliate our families and end up in prison and ruin our lives because if we ever got out, no one good would have anything to do with us again."

It boggled me that he'd managed to make it about them

and *their* lives, when they'd so callously pulled apart someone else's. I'd hoped Peyton would do the right thing, but Jonathan's influence clearly outweighed mine and Joseph's.

"So how are you going to make this right?" Sabrina asked coldly.

A shrug. "I wanted to talk. To tell you I'm sorry things got so out of control. And—"

"You're *sorry*. You think that's enough?" she interrupted.

Peyton's face reddened. "I don't know what else there is. I can't go back in time and fix things. What else is there?"

"You could tell the truth."

"How will that help anyone? It doesn't undo what happened." He held up a hand. "Why should our lives be ruined, too?" he asked.

When I had first met Peyton and Jonathan, Peyton had seemed far more sympathetic. Now, I suspected he was no better than Jonathan with his bluster. They were different sides of the same privileged coin: complicity and utter denial.

I saw Missy walk up to Sabrina. I had no idea why, and I probably couldn't have reacted in time to stop what came next anyway. I will forever regret that I didn't try.

Sabrina lifted her right arm, and I saw the spark from her hand a moment before the bullet entered Peyton. He let out a cry of pain, dropped to his knees, and put his hands over his stomach.

Blood dripped from Peyton's shirt, steaming on the sidewalk as it met icy stone. Time slowed again.

I saw Sabrina lift the gun a second time.

"Sabrina, NO!" I cried out as I lunged forward.

Andre caught me and carried me away from the trio.

But Sabrina stopped. She stared at Peyton for a long moment and dropped the weapon.

"Sabrina!" Missy called out.

Sabrina shook her head.

Thank God, I thought.

But I watched in horror as Missy ran toward Peyton, who was scrambling to get away. I barely saw the flash of the blade, and I began screaming and scrambling to loosen Andre's hold as the gleaming metal went into Peyton's back.

He fell onto his left side on the cement. The knife was still sticking out of his body, blood pumping out of him onto the cold pavement.

Finally Missy gave Andre a nod, and he let me go. I rushed forward, putting a finger to Peyton's throat to see if I could feel a pulse. I was too nervous to tell for sure. I knew not to remove the blade, which could have caused him to bleed out.

His eyes were open, but they didn't seem to register anything. I held his hand and tried to whisper something comforting. "Just stay here. It's going to be all right, Peyton. It's Christmas." It was all nonsense.

"Someone should call an ambulance," I muttered with numb lips.

"Why don't you, Grandma?" Missy taunted. "If you trust the authorities so much."

I saw the hardness in her eyes. All I could feel was the same sense of helplessness I'd always felt in the face of death. Georgia's, yes, but all the others I'd encountered, too. My sleuthing couldn't save anyone. I had never been in control here.

I sought out Sabrina's face. Tears were dripping down it. But then she said, "I had to do it, Linda. I told you, I couldn't be the victim anymore. I had to be the one to make things change."

Yes, she had.

I looked back at Peyton and imagined his parents' grief. No parent should experience the loss of their child this way, even if that child had done horrible things. Why hadn't I been able to stop this? All sense of the divine had left me.

Oh, Peyton. Oh, Sabrina. Oh, Missy.

Someone else must have called an ambulance, maybe the convenience store clerk, because in a few minutes, one pulled into the parking lot. The EMTs hopped out and started working on Peyton, hooking him up to an IV and putting him into the back of the ambulance before driving off.

Wait—did that mean he was alive?

In the gap between that moment and the police arriving, Sabrina came over and put her bloodstained hands in mine.

"Can you take me home now?" she whispered. "I'll do whatever you ask me to. I just want to be with you on Christmas."

She hugged me again, like she had last night. I patted her back, but I'd never felt further away from another person.

She went on. "She told me I had to do this in order to get myself back. To live without being afraid."

I said nothing but sat there with her until the police arrived.

CHAPTER 27

I couldn't leave until the police took our statements. It seemed everyone else had already given them the details by the time they got to me. I didn't know what I could add.

"Did you see her shoot the gun?" asked the detective, who looked as cold as I felt. Snow was falling more heavily now, enough to stick to the roads.

When they were younger, the boys would have called this the perfect Christmas morning. The sun was starting to rise behind the mountains, lighting up the clouds and making the falling snow look like red jewels floating in the sky. It was the thick sort of snow that would be perfect for making snowmen. Or snow angels.

"Mrs. Wallheim, did you see her shoot the gun?" the detective repeated.

I must have told him my name at some point, but I didn't remember doing it. Or was it Sabrina who had told him?

"Yes," I said, before he asked again. "And I saw the knife go in afterward." I held out my hands, still stained with Peyton's blood.

Red was a Christmas color. To remind us of Christ's blood,

shed for us on the cross. Red and white candy canes. Red velvet ribbons on the tree. The red winking lights of Temple Square, which I could see, even from here. Or was that just in my head?

"Is he alive?"

"Critical condition. Did you hear the argument? About a rape accusation?"

"Yes," I said dully.

I'd been to the trial for Carrie Helm's killer. I'd testified very briefly about her relationship with her husband and her father. I knew how the defense treated a prosecution's witness. But I couldn't imagine testifying against Sabrina. Or Missy. They were so young and had been through so much.

"It isn't fair," I said out loud.

"No, it's not. It's always hard to see a young person grievously injured. And in a case like this, you always feel like you could've stopped it, I guess," said the detective. It was an attempt to be kind. But he didn't understand. At least three lives had been irrevocably changed by the events of the last two weeks.

I began to sob as I saw a detective tuck a blanket around Sabrina. At least someone was treating her as she deserved to be treated, for now.

I couldn't see Missy anywhere. Had they already taken her away?

How could it be Christmas morning? I felt a like stranger in my own body, completely hollowed out. I didn't know where to go or what to do.

Someone had phoned Kurt because he appeared right after the detective walked off. I sat on the cold wet cement without even a plastic bag underneath me.

I'd felt his presence somehow, even before he called my name and ran toward me.

He flung his arms around me, no word of recrimination. Not yet, anyway.

"Let's get you home. It looks like you're free to go." He glanced around, and no one stopped us as he led me away.

"What about Jonathan?" I asked.

"He's safe at home. The police checked on him after Peyton went to the hospital," Kurt said.

That wasn't what I meant. "Did you bring my phone?" I asked.

Kurt held it up. He must have seen it on my nightstand and grabbed it for me, bless him.

I went back to the detective I'd just spoken to. It took some insistence to get him to listen to me. My words were disjointed, and my mouth felt numb. Maybe he thought I was hysterical, but finally he listened to the recorded confession.

"I see," he said.

"Will it make a difference?" I asked. "For Sabrina and Missy."

He looked up at Kurt, two men speaking without words, as if I wasn't even there. Then he turned back to me. "It will be useful to clarify the reason for the attack," he said, tapping on my phone, presumably to send the recording to someone official.

"But what about the rape? Won't there be a trial for that?" I demanded breathlessly.

"Possibly," he said. "But it's going to be difficult for someone accused of attempted murder to pursue this. It will be all too easy to argue that she made up the accusation to justify the attack."

But it *was* what had caused the attack. It wasn't some theoretical justification.

Looking back, Detective Gore's words seemed like a warning. One that I, yet again, had refused to heed. I shouldn't have promised Sabrina justice or hidden the evidence I'd had from her. She'd stopped trusting everyone else, so she'd decided to take action on her own. A fifteen-year-old girl, trying to make the world listen to her. And in the end, she would be seen as the villain, not the victim.

Unlike those good Mormon boys, I thought again.

I started sobbing, and Kurt pulled me back toward the car.

I stared at my phone between us in his truck, wondering how things would be different if I'd never recorded that confession. Or if I'd never given her the money that I was almost certainly sure she'd used to buy that gun. I had hoped to protect her, but perhaps this tragedy would have come to pass no matter what.

"Maybe there will be two trials. They could still charge Peyton and Jonathan and the others," Kurt said.

But I'd given up hope for that, just as Sabrina had. Getting justice seemed infinitely more difficult now.

Kurt drove, patting my hand gently now and again.

"The boys will be home soon," he said.

The next thing I remembered, we were home, and Kurt was guiding me upstairs.

"Dinner," I said. "I have to make dinner." My sons would be here in just a few hours. It was my job as their mother to make Christmas dinner. I'd failed in so many ways as a mother today; I couldn't fail at this.

But Kurt shook his head as he tucked me into bed. "Don't

worry about anything. I'll handle dinner, Linda. You sleep for now. I'll wake you up when the boys arrive."

My daughter was gone, and I hadn't saved Sabrina, either. I'd tried everything, but she'd slipped away from me, too.

CHAPTER 28

Kurt woke me around one that afternoon, and I could already hear the sounds downstairs, including squeals from Carla.

"They're all here," he said.

"Did they start opening already?" I asked. My body felt heavy and sore all over, but at least I was physically present, my mind clearer than it had been before. The morning's events no longer seemed like a dream.

"Linda? Do you want to take a shower first?"

I looked down at myself, still in the pajamas I'd worn under my coat when I'd left to find Sabrina in the middle of the night. Kurt must have thrown out the bloodstained coat.

"Yes," I got out, my mind circling back to the question at hand.

"We'll wait for you, then. I promise, no one will do any opening until you're there to watch. Okay?" Kurt still had that tone in his voice, as if I might break into pieces at any moment.

I didn't blame him. I wasn't sure myself, but I put out a hand and touched his shoulder. "I'm here," I said. "I'm back."

"You are?" He looked at me for several seconds.

I was feeling more myself again, which meant it was time for an apology. "I'm sorry," I said. "I know I shouldn't have just gone out like that last night. I'm not sure why I did." I couldn't even come up with an excuse. My emotions had washed away, leaving me empty and searching.

"You keep doing this, Linda. Putting yourself in danger. Lying to me, keeping me out of the loop, then expecting me to help clean up."

"I know," I admitted, though I still wasn't quite sure why or how to fix it.

"You always promise you'll stop."

"I know," I said again. But was that what I really wanted?

"I don't know if I can keep living like this. It feels like I have no control over my own life anymore. You make all the decisions for both of us, and I'm left trying to guess what's coming next and how to shield us all from the consequences," Kurt said.

He thought *I* was the one in control? If so, I wasn't doing a very good job at it.

"Not right now?" I said softly.

"Fine," he said, though I knew this would be coming up in therapy.

For now, I just had to get through today. I closed the bathroom door.

I showered quickly and went downstairs to a different world. I watched Carla figure out how to open presents agonizingly slowly, Joseph and Willow constantly having to help. As I'd expected, she found the paper itself as delightful as anything beneath it.

Kenneth and Naomi were there with Talitha, their adopted

daughter. She showed off a new scarf, diaphanous silk in greenish blue, and a new pair of earrings.

"My mom would never have let me get my ears pierced before," she said, showing off her untouched lobes. "But Naomi set up a free appointment for me at the mall. She says they promise it won't even hurt." She smiled at her older sister.

"You're a tough cookie," said Naomi, hugging her.

I winced, remembering that I'd said the same thing to Sabrina. But here was my real family. My sons. And they had no idea what had happened.

Zachary poked his head upstairs at some point, then came back down to ask why his room was so clean.

"We had a guest," Kurt answered simply.

Dinner wasn't terrible, I could give Kurt that. He'd gone out and bought rolls while I was asleep. The potatoes were flakes and triaged with plenty of butter and cream, though still tasteless in my book. There were sweet potatoes but plain out of the oven with no fancy toppings. The turkey wasn't too dry, though it wasn't particularly pretty. Someone had told Kurt to cook it upside down, which ruined the skin, but it did keep the juices in.

Naomi and Willow had worked together to make pies in the short time frame Kurt must have given them. Naomi's crust was perfect, though the filling was a little tart, and Willow's crust was overworked, but I gave only compliments to my daughters-in-law. Maybe they'd help more with Christmas dinner next year, if I let them.

Later, Kurt organized the boys into two groups, one to clear the table and wrap up leftovers, the other to rinse dishes and put them in the dishwasher, the excess sitting in a pile next to the sink.

I sat in the living room and stared out the window.

"Mom, are you all right?" asked Naomi.

"Yes," I said reflexively. "Don't worry, I'm fine."

After a pause, I asked, "Naomi, do you still believe in God?" She'd left her own family's fundamentalist brand of Mormonism, and Kenneth had left his. I knew it wasn't the kind of thing I should have been asking on Christmas. But I wanted to know.

She looked wistful. "No, not really. I wish I did, though. It seems like it would be nice to believe that He's holding things up somehow, that eventually it will all work out."

Naomi drifted away a moment later, when Talitha called her over to help her set up the digital camera that Kurt and I had bought her.

Then we headed to the computer Adam had set up in the front room so we could all talk to Samuel at once. Only then did I realize Adam's wife, Marie, wasn't here. No one had mentioned her absence. Were she and Adam having trouble?

I shook my head to try to get any bad thoughts out. This was Christmas. It was supposed to be a day of peace and joy.

Then Samuel appeared on the screen in a suit and tie. It was the most beautiful thing I'd ever seen.

I started crying immediately, and Kurt handed me the box of tissues he had thoughtfully brought in ahead of time.

"How are you, son?" he asked.

"I'm great, Dad. I'm in Maynard now, and the people here are so friendly. The Carringtons invited us over for dinner, and they have investigators coming in a couple of hours to talk about baptism dates. I have a good feeling about my place here." His voice sounded different. Stronger. Happier. Was it real or to put on a good face?

"And your new companion?" asked Kurt.

Samuel thumped a vague shoulder, then pulled a new face into the picture. It was a young Chinese man who smiled and waved to us. "Good to meet you," he said with a slight accent. "This is Elder Hong," he said. "He and I are going to be awesome together."

I found myself relaxing at Samuel's superlatives. I focused on his face, expressive and full of light. He turned to Zachary and laughed at a joke one of them had cracked—probably Zachary.

Kurt thumped Zachary on the back, then shook a finger at him.

Joseph showed off Carla's new skill—she could take three steps on her own without falling.

Sabrina wasn't here to see it. She might never see Carla again. Or Joseph or Willow or any of us. And I had to make peace with that and move on with what I had. Who I had. I was a mother to five wonderful sons. This was enough.

I noticed Willow was talking to Naomi off to the side, probably comparing notes on their two husbands.

Kenneth was talking to Samuel about how he was doing, skirting his disapproval of the way the Mormon Church treated gay people.

I looked over at Adam, alone, his hands folded obediently into his lap as if he were in Primary again. My mother's intuition told me something was wrong. He was following the conversation dimly, as I was, but not participating in it. The pie he had picked at was on a plate by his side. If he moved even slightly, it would topple to the floor. But he was constrained in everything he did.

Had he and Marie had a fight this morning? Or last night? I'd ask him about it, but not today. There had been enough pain this Christmas. But part of me was grateful that even as adults, my sons still needed me sometimes.

"Linda, do you want to say goodbye to Samuel?" Kurt asked me, nudging me with his arm.

"Bye, Samuel!" I said, smiling and waving to him. My mouth felt achy, as if I'd been chewing taffy all day.

Then the screen went dark, and we all paused for a moment, taking a breath before heading back to the kitchen.

I thought about going on a walk outside. I wanted to get away from the boisterous noise in the kitchen: my sons teasing each other and wrestling with their father. I didn't think I'd get very far, though. The thought of the cold and the weight of my own legs held me back.

Finally, Willow came to sit by me.

"Joseph got a text a few minutes ago," she said quietly. "From Sabrina's parents."

"Oh," I said. Why hadn't I called them myself? I should have. But to tell them what? That I'd seen the incident that would take their daughter from them for years, but I hadn't stopped it?

I thought of all the choices I'd made the last two weeks. If I had refused to come up when Joseph asked me to or given up my search for Sabrina at the library or had her father take her home when he'd stormed up to my house, the outcome might have been different, though there was no guarantee of that.

"Peyton's going to be okay," Willow said.

I reached for her hand and held it, breathing relief.

"But Sabrina and Missy are going to be tried as adults for attempted murder," she added.

"Oh, God," I whispered.

"Her parents want me and Joseph to testify for her. But they're asking you to stay away from the case," Willow went on.

I looked at her. "I can try, but I don't know if that's possible," I said, since I'd been a witness to the incident.

"Yeah," she breathed out. "I know." She put a hand on my shoulder. "It's tough, but it's going to be okay."

PEYTON RECOVERED FULLY from his injuries, though when I saw him at the trial, he looked gaunt and completely changed from the young man he had been. In the end, Missy was sentenced to five years in adult prison, having turned eighteen just days before the incident. Sabrina went to a juvenile detention facility until she was eighteen. Neither Jonathan nor Peyton ever went to trial for rape. The only punishment they faced was not going on their missions, as far as I could tell.

Kurt and I went to marriage therapy week after week, him angry as ever, me biting my tongue. The church went on, too, probably telling more victims it was their own fault for dressing immodestly or making excuses for their abusers who were important as priesthood holders to the church— shouldn't we think about their lives, too?

And I didn't know what it meant to be Mormon anymore or if I wanted to be one. It would cost me everything, it seemed, if I walked away. Everything except myself.